BOURBON PENN

30

August 2023

Bourbon Penn Issue 30

August 2023

Copyright © 2023 by Cognitive Wave, Inc.

www.bourbonpenn.com

Myrtle Beach, SC

Editor:

Erik Secker

Copy Editing:

J. Scott Wilson

Cover Art:

The Real Winnie

copyright © by Bom.K

Very special thanks to:
*George Tom Elavathingal, Jen Lin,
Ioanna Papadopoulou, and Sam Rebelein*

"The Demon Lord of Broken Concrete" copyright © 2023 by Alex Irvine

"Polar Shift" copyright © 2023 by Mir Seidel

"Bachelard Forgets the Kitchen" copyright © 2023 by Cedrick May

"Strange Eons" copyright © 2023 by Keira Perkins

"Partial Transcript from The Great Brexit Baking Show" copyright © 2023 by Rich Larson

"It Tastes of Rot" copyright © 2023 by Margaret Roach

"Clown's Balloons" copyright © 2023 by Sam Rebelein

CONTENTS

THE DEMON LORD OF BROKEN CONCRETE   7
Alex Irvine

POLAR SHIFT   31
Mir Seidel

BACHELARD FORGETS THE KITCHEN   49
Cedrick May

STRANGE EONS   65
Keira Perkins

PARTIAL TRANSCRIPT FROM THE GREAT BREXIT BAKING SHOW   85
Rich Larson

IT TASTES OF ROT   101
Margaret Roach

CLOWN'S BALLOONS   127
Sam Rebelein

THE DEMON LORD OF BROKEN CONCRETE

■

Alex Irvine

He was always there when Zack walked to school. Tall, stoop-shouldered, reddish hair in his eyes but cut short around the ears and neck. A slow kid, not slow enough to be on the short bus but he goes to special classes. He's a few years older, been held back some. Lives in a house full of foster kids. Maybe is one himself. Zack doesn't know. The kid's name is Tim but when the sidewalks along Hewitt Road are full of kids walking to Ypsi High—down the hill past the church, back up past the soccer field and in the back door if it's open, all the way around to the front if it's not—his name is rarely used. Kids fear his kind of difference.

Zack talks to him, though, at least when there isn't anyone else around, and he always says hi even when the other kids don't. He feels a little bad for the kid, who doesn't seem to have any friends beyond the other foster kids. Tim is friendly but a little cautious. People are mean to him a lot. Zack sympathizes. High school is hard enough without people giving you shit while you're walking to school. What does it cost you to be kind? Nothing, except the way kindness makes you a target for people who suffered for being kind, and now must pass that suffering on.

Then one day they don't see Tim on Hewitt Road, and after a week they realize they haven't seen him in a while, and then they hear that a guy down by the dam snagging bullhead has found his body. For a few days nobody says what happened, but Zack already knows. Tim didn't get over there by himself.

Do you believe in God? Sometimes Zack and his friends ask each other this question. They all have different answers, and their answers are always changing. Zack believes that there is more than one god, and that different gods rule over different people. Kids like him, all of them worshipped the Demon Lord of Broken Concrete whether they knew it or not. That was the answer Zack never gave, but the truth of it was all around.

The gods of these children do not hold sway over the harvest, or cats, or thunder. They are the Marquess of Daddy's Eighth Beer, Our Lady of What Did You Just Say to Me?, He Who Reigns over White Panel Vans, Our Lord of Kindly Men Who Want to Show You a Puppy, the Archfiend of This Will Hurt Me More Than It Hurts You, the Earl of The Looks You Get When You Use Food Stamps at the Grocery Store, the Duke of Home from School to an Empty Fridge. The Demon Lord of Broken Concrete rules them all. His chief lieutenants are the Viscount of Rust and the Baroness of Shattered Glass.

Zack learned this in church, although the way he thinks about it is equal parts New Testament and *Deities and Demigods*. It is a logical consequence of sin that there should be demons as well as God, and demons are essentially of the same nature as God, because they all rule over something. He has never been able to explain this logic to anyone, but in his mind it is as solid as a dam. Everything else he knows must flow either around or over it.

It is possible to catch glimpses of the Demon Lord of Broken Concrete. All you have to do is be in the right place at the right time, and understand that the world is bigger than you will ever know and that you cannot control anything beyond what you can put your hands on, and often not even that. You have to live in a place that is dying and knows it is dying. You have to surround yourselves with other kids who know they missed the boat to catch the American Dream, most of them, because it's not in Ypsi anymore. The plants are going dark, the people are doing what desperate people do. The Demon Lord of Broken Concrete reigns over places such as this and is well pleased.

His parents don't really care where he goes as long as he's home for dinner, so Zack goes as far as his bike will take him when it's not soccer season. A few weeks ago, he rode down a newly bulldozed road through a brushy field, with a big sign out front announcing the subdivision to be built. *Your New Home for 1984!* There was a battered old Ford pickup at the end of the road, and two kids next to it, one about his age and one a little older. They both had BB guns and they showed him a row of dead birds on the dropped tailgate. Sparrows, robins, cardinals, blue jays, other birds Zack didn't recognize. For weeks afterward,

Zack's dreams were full of death. Worms growing pale in mud puddles, a caterpillar smashed on the sidewalk and a little girl skipping away from it laughing, a cat his father had run over in a parking lot by accident and then backed over again to make sure it wasn't suffering.

Death is everywhere, and the Demon Lord of Broken Concrete favors children.

Today he's down by the lake, his bike hidden in some bushes growing up along the fence surrounding a ruined old factory. Henry Ford built it, but it's changed hands a lot since then. Now it's rusting metal, shards of glass, cracked bricks. Broken concrete. He doesn't go inside, he's got enough survival instinct for that at least, but he finds a hole in the fence and kicks around the property, picking up rocks and throwing them at other rocks. There aren't even any rats because there's nothing within a mile that a rat could eat.

This is the east side, the domain of angry factory rats, the human kind. Heavy metal, Confederate flags, babies born knowing how to bleed brake lines. The west side is where the professionals live, close to the college and the rarefied air of Ann Arbor. The south side is historically black, but there are plenty of black people in Zack's neighborhood, which is on the south side of the west side. Zack's parents always look for places on the west side, because they are aspirational on their children's behalf. That's how they landed on Hewitt Road, which puts Zack in the preferred schools but is still cheap because it's on the edge of the township.

The factory is partially torn down. In ruins like these, anything can happen because the past has been destroyed and the future still might never happen. This is the realm of the Fallen Angels of Bent Rebar, the lesser hosts of dirt clods and gravel in your eyes, the Principalities of Lonely Plants Dying by Themselves in the Tracks of Backhoes. These are lesser aspects of the Demon Lord of Broken Concrete.

The catechism of the Demon Lord of Broken Concrete is this: Fuckin' Japs. Fuckin' immigrants. Fuckin' OPEC. Fuckin' EPA. In Zack's mind, the Demon Lord of Broken Concrete has a face like Ronald Reagan if Reagan was on a Hammer horror movie poster as the monstrous villain. No, Lee Iacocca. A late-night special too soul-suckingly terrifying for even the Ghoul to introduce.

A concrete chip about the size of a taco spins through the air over his head and lands out in the weedy parking lot.

He ducks in close to the rubble pile, not sure if someone is throwing concrete at him or just throwing it and hasn't noticed him. One time at another place like this, a chunk of concrete fell from on high, out of the sun. Zack scrambled on the rubble, tearing up his knees. A piece of rebar dug into his right ankle. Once there was order here. Something was falling from the sky to bring order once more. The chunk of concrete struck him on the back of the head and for a moment he couldn't see, there was a ringing in his ears and he felt like he was staring into the sun even though he was face down in the rubble and weeds. His little brother JJ found him like that, and started to cry, saying I'm sorry I'm sorry over and over again. It's okay, Zack said. I know you didn't do it on purpose. He didn't say that JJ couldn't have done it on purpose. His hand was guided. These are the immutable laws of the construction site, the abandoned building, the overgrown field with an old basement foundation still visible in one corner. The path under the bridge, the cinder embankment by the railroad tracks. These are the haunts of the Demon Lord of Broken Concrete and his innumerable host. Anyone who sets foot in those spaces, especially a child, and most especially a child whose kindness and empathy is a closely held secret—that child is what the Demon Lord of Broken Concrete prizes above all else.

And now it is happening again, only it isn't JJ whose face pops up over the debris pile. It's a black kid Zack vaguely knows from history class, maybe? Something about him is familiar, anyway. But he can't remember the kid's name. They stand there looking at each other, each with a chunk of concrete dangling in one hand.

Hey, the kid says. Bet you can't throw as far as me.

Bet I can. Zack has a pretty good arm, and what's the point of giving up before you try? Zack always tries, even when he knows he's going to lose.

They both throw. The concrete pieces land pretty close together.

Let's do it again, the kid says.

Zack's already getting another chunk of concrete.

Six or eight throws in they're pretty evenly matched. What's your name? Zack asks.

Ro, the kid says. Meaning Roosevelt.

Ro what?

Ro McPherson.

It all comes together. You Elvin McPherson's brother? I sat next to him in like third grade.

Ro's eyes cut away, toward the empty ruin. Yeah. Elvin's in jail. Probly for a long time. He's quiet for a little while after that. Neither of them throws again.

The Demon Lord of Broken Concrete dislikes human connection. He will not permit it in the spaces he rules. He finds your pain, and uses it to pit you against other people. Now Zack and Ro are facing each other like strangers again, each with a chunk of concrete in their hands.

I gotta go, Zack says, before something happens. He drops the chunk. Good throws.

Yeah, you too, says Roosevelt. He's still on top of the debris pile when Zack gets on his bike, still throwing chunk after chunk out over the weedy expanse of asphalt. Then as Zack rides away, he hears the first crash as Ro turns his attention to the factory's remaining windows.

Dang, Zack thinks. I should have stayed.

About a week after they killed Tim, word started to get around about how they did it. The tellings are like campfire stories, ghoulish, darkly gleeful. Zack doesn't know if anyone else feels the same way, but they leave him emptied out. If he has to have feelings in those moments, they're going to be feelings he can't handle. So he has no feelings.

It was a sacrifice. He knows this. Gods demand sacrifices. This sacrifice was lured into a car with the offer of a ride, then taken to a house where unspecified rituals were performed. This sacrifice was given enough whiskey to give him alcohol poisoning. This sacrifice was then taken to the river, just below the dam, at the old boat ramp with algae in its concrete grooves and drowned. But he did not die, so this sacrifice was stabbed until the air he would not let out of his mouth bubbled up from the wounds in his back.

Nobody knows why. But Zack knows why. It was a sacrifice. It could have been any of them, any of the kids who walk down Hewitt Road every morning to school and then in the afternoons range across the city's empty lots and construction sites, alleys and empty schoolyards and garages. Nobody cares where they are or what they do, until they do something wrong.

He imagines dying face down at the boat launch, the last thing he ever sees the crumbling concrete sloping away into darkness.

There's a rumor that Robbie Grabowski got caught fucking a dog and that's why he hasn't been in school in a while. Zack's cousin Clayton was friends with Robbie when they were in elementary school, so Zack and Clayton go over there to see if they can find out if it's true. Not like they're just going to ask him, but they'll see what they can see.

The Grabowski house is between the college and a strip of old foundries and machine shops off Huron River Drive where it runs past the old paper mill. The houses here are all the same, little ranches with one-car garages punctuated by the occasional Victorian farmhouse from back before Ypsi industrialized. The farmhouses are all chopped up into apartments. From Robbie Grabowski's front yard, you can see the smokestacks of the paper mill and the ruin of what used to be the Ypsilanti Underwear Company. Zack is always tickled to remember that Ypsi underwear used to be famously durable.

Clayton knocks on the door. Robbie's mother answers. Hello, Clayton. Gosh, it's been a while since we saw you around here. She looks just like him, red hair and freckles and weak chin. Zack doesn't know Robbie too well, but he doesn't like the idea of people spreading rumors about anybody. It's happened to him, and it feels shitty.

Yeah, um, we haven't seen Robbie around in a while so, um, we were cruising by and thought we'd see what was up.

She sees right through him. Robert isn't here, she says stiffly. And you haven't— She looks back into the house. Shakes her head. Looks back at Clayton, and now she's afraid. It's nice of you to stop by. I'll tell Robert. Just before she shuts the door, she adds I remember when you were such good friends.

Man, that was weird, Zack says when they're walking back toward the college campus. Did you see her? She looked scared.

I'd be scared too if I had to live with Robbie Grabowski, Clayton says. There's an ugly tone in his voice Zack doesn't remember hearing before. Shit, it might be true, Clayton says. He snorts out a laugh. At least that's what I'm going to say if anybody asks.

Not cool, Zack says. He feels like the whole thing has blown up in his face.

Clayton shrugs and starts walking. Who cares?

Zack does. But now there's nothing he can do. He's sad because he and Clayton were always close, and Clayton didn't use to have this mean streak. You can't help who you're related to.

To get back to Clayton's house, where they're going to kill the afternoon playing Atari, they cut along the backtracks. It's an old railroad spur, some paved and some dirt. Homeless people camp in the brush on either side, and kids find spaces to smoke cigarettes they stole from the

Stop-n-Go and drink beers from their dad's basement fridge.

They're behind one of the apartment complexes by the college when they see a bunch of kids aiming a garden hose into a trash can. Little kids, eleven or twelve. Zack is fourteen. One of them has a stick. He's poking it down in the can. Water splashes out. They look up and see Zack and Clayton. We got a woodchuck, one of them says. We're drownding it. Come here. Pretty soon you can see the bubbles coming up. Zack doesn't know what Clayton is going to do, but he gets out of there. He can't be there for that much pain. The animal's pain and terror, the pain those boys have suffered that becomes a living thing inside them that has to get out. Like Zack's dad. Like the kids who threw rocks at him when he and Godfrey Nabalinde were on their bikes riding to Godfrey's house, down in the South Side. Hey man, ain't you in the wrong neighborhood? Godfrey shaking his head, saying Shit, they could mean me. Because he's African. He runs into shitstorms Zack can't even imagine. That pain is a god, and all of those boys are its living avatars. The Demon Lord of Broken Concrete binds his people in service, forbids them a life beyond the life that was taken from them when the plant closed.

The guys who killed Tim tried to drown him. But when he didn't die fast enough, they got out their knives. At least that's the story.

He's been making out with this girl named Penny, mostly in the stairwell behind the pool balcony in the last few minutes of lunch period. One day out of the blue she says if he comes over to her house before her mom gets home from work on Friday, she'll give him a blowjob. So he does, and she does. She's never done it before and one time when she comes up for air, he can't help himself, he's coming. She bursts out laughing and then clamps both hands over her mouth and runs to the bathroom for a towel. She throws it at him, still laughing, bright red. After a while, he can't help but laugh too. Hey, he offers, do you want me to...? He's never done it before and he's curious what it would be like, but she's worried her mom will be home soon, so she takes a rain check. He's late for soccer practice. The coach, a Portuguese psychopath who doesn't care whether the team wins or loses as long as the players suffer, has him running sprints up the hill behind the high school until Zack thinks he's going to puke. But he won't let the coach see him do it.

Something about the way Penny laughed makes the Demon Lord of Broken Concrete feel far away, just for a little while.

The next Tuesday there's an away game. Zack gets to the bus pickup early, after doing some homework in the choir room until the janitors kick him out. The only other person waiting for the bus so early is Tommy Keenan, who sits on the curb tapping a Coke bottle on the concrete. You hear about Tim? Zack asks. Tommy doesn't know who Tim is. He's from the east side, they all bus or drive to the high school. But since Zack brought it up, Tommy's interested. Who is he? A kid in my neighborhood, Zack says. I guess he got killed.

A group of girls walks by, feathered hair and Jordache and halter tops, Marlboros sticking out of their purses. Tommy says hi to one of them. She says hi back. I'd like to get up on top of her and fuck her between her tits, he says to Zack after they're gone, tapping the bottle harder. It breaks, and a bright line of blood appears on his thumb. Shit, he says. He goes looking for some Band-Aids and the rest of the team is there by the time he gets back. The bus pulls up. The whole ride to the game, Zack is thinking, you can do that?

As it happens, Tommy's blood is a sacrifice. They beat a team they're not supposed to beat, and Tommy scores the winning goal. None of their parents are in the stands, but they don't think much about it. It's an away game.

The team is scrappy but only the immigrant kids really know how to play. There's Phuc from Vietnam, who starts a fight with anybody who calls him Fuck. Zikri from Malaysia, Hung from China, Eduardo from Guatemala, Godfrey from Uganda, Christian the exchange student from Denmark. Their goalie is an East Side kid named Greg, all attitude and veiny lean muscle. Zack could almost be gay for those veins, what does a guy have to do to get veins like those. Greg's a great athlete, has no idea how to play soccer, but he gets the kamikaze part of goalkeeping pretty fast, so he plays a lot. Zack isn't gay, even though he let Phil Briscoe press his cock up against his belly a couple of times when they were like eleven or twelve, pretending they knew what sex was. He remembers the heat of it, the way it throbbed. There's a story that the guys who killed Tim made him do that, too, but Zack doesn't know.

His Dad and Uncle Roy take Zack and Clayton bass fishing out at the old quarry. They're not catching anything, and Zack gets bored. He and Clayton swim out to the craggy little island in the middle of the quarry. There are machines down deep in the water, and of course those have demonic rulers too. If you can't see the demonic energy in the clawed bucket of a backhoe, reaching up toward sunlight from two hundred feet underwater, you're just blind, is all. Grownups can't see it. Zack thinks he's going to work that into a D&D campaign sometime. Demonic machines rising from black water, there would be a wizard behind it, some kind of lich maybe like in *Tomb of Horrors* ...

He tries to tell Clayton about Tim, but Clayton doesn't want to talk about it. He plays tennis, his dad's a Vietnam vet who likes to antagonize people, they have enough money that they're going to Germany that summer. He's on the edges of different circles than the ones Zack runs in, and he doesn't have time for some special-ed kid who got himself into trouble. That's how Uncle Roy characterized Tim's murder the one time it came up among the adults.

Clayton needs to take a shit but there's no toilet paper. "Man, my butt's going to itch for the rest of my life," he moans. Zack suggests leaves but there aren't any leaves on this hump of rock, at least not any big enough to work, and Clayton is worried about poison ivy. So he's going to have to clean himself in the water, and no way is Zack standing around for that even though Clayton is scared to swim by himself. Truth is, Zack is too, but this is his private, unknowable revenge for Clayton being a dick about Robbie Grabowski. He swims back to shore, certain at every moment that a backhoe bucket is going to reach up out of the darkness and scoop him down where he belongs. When he feels the mucky shoreline between his toes, it's like he's accomplished something.

A year goes by. Robbie Grabowski comes back to school. He was down in Tennessee with relatives, staying out of his dad's way. Some kid mentions the dog thing to him, and Robbie kicks the shit out of him. Case closed. Zack wishes it was Clayton who had said it, and Clayton who got his ass beat, and then he feels bad about that because you're not supposed to think things like that about family.

In freezing cold and steamy heat, rain or snow, they walk down the hill on Hewitt Road. Zack sees a girl he likes, Trina, but she doesn't talk to him. He runs into another guy on the soccer team, Kirk, but Kirk doesn't talk to him either. Kirk and Trina walk right in front of him talking. This is where Tim would always be, too, sometimes talking to Darryl Paquette, sometimes talking to Zack. Mostly walking alone. Zack mostly walks alone, too.

He gets his driver's license and his dad gives him a car. Not two weeks later he gets in an argument, things escalate, and his dad chases him out of the house. Zack's standing there in the street, shorts, no shirt, no wallet, no nothing. His dad walks over to the car, pops the hood, rips out the spark plug wires. Holds them up like a trophy with a gleam in his eye. Walks back in the house and lets the screen door slam behind him.

JJ brings him a shirt and some shoes, and Zack takes off. He can't find any of his friends and doesn't really feel like talking about it anyway, so he spends most of the night in one of the dugouts over at the Little League field in Candy Cane Park. This is the same park where Scottie Bauman sometimes used to bring Sherri Friedel to make out. Sherri Friedel is so fantastically hot that whenever people see Scottie's orange Gremlin, they skulk around hoping to see her through the windows. Zack never did this, but he has undertaken his own devotions to Sherri Friedel.

The mosquitoes aren't too bad. When he figures everyone must be asleep, he heads back to the house, watches carefully for a while to be sure, then sneaks in his bedroom window.

・・・

A few days later, they're all pretending everything is normal. It wasn't even like the last time, where Zack got up the next morning and his dad was sitting on the couch. I'm sorry I slugged you, he said, and that was supposed to be the end of it. But he still had to go to school, see people eyeing the bruises, hear Deedee Fields say, I heard what happened, Zack, I'm so sorry. She's a great soul, Deedee, but Zack doesn't want anyone to be sorry for him. He mumbles something along the lines of thanks and puts his head down for the rest of the day. His face hurts. Everyone can see it.

Could. Could, could, that's not now, that was last year. The last bad one. In between, just sporadic moments where Zack felt like things could go sideways real fast. It would be easier if his dad was a monster, but he's not. He gives everything he has. Wednesdays at Taco Bell where Zack eats five Tacos Bell Grande, wrestling matches in the yard, teaching Zack how to change the Mustang's oil or build a Pinewood Derby car or sing along with the harmony parts in the songs on the radio. Even the Kinks which is gay rock according to his dad, but he sings along anyway. He doesn't know anything about soccer, but when

Zack is into it, he learns. They talk about books, since Dad is a big fan of old sci-fi and fantasy. Dad taught Zack to play D&D, and what other kid could say that.

But then there was the time when he knocked you out cold in the McDonald's because he didn't like something you'd said to Mom. Or the times when you were hanging out with a new friend on the street, and went to his house, down in the basement, to look at his Micronauts. Mom couldn't find you, and because Mom was scared, Dad got the belt out. The sound of the leather rasping free of his belt loops in the basement, that's a small god all by itself, a godling of dread and memory who serves at the right hand of the Demon Lord of Broken Concrete. It's not as bad as what Dad suffered when he was a kid, so mostly it's all right. Zack understands that he is a sacrifice to the older god his father carries, just as his father was offered up to propitiate the gods who rode his father along the hobo railroads from the Upper Peninsula down to Detroit, and then to war and back, and then to Ypsi. It has to be a god or a demon, because it can't be just people.

His dad needed Zack to understand how badly he had been hurt, and his only way of saying it was to pass that pain along. Maybe he even meant it as a warning—see what the world will do to you?—and he had no other way to say it. But if that was the case, Zack thought, he had it figured out already. He knew that in middle school, when Eddie Brooks showed up on their front porch with a gun, coked up and still pissed about a fight he and Zack had gotten into in fifth grade. And if that hadn't gotten the message across, Zack knew it when Eddie killed a guy in the Stop-n-Go parking lot over a girl they'd both been dating. That was the year after Tim was murdered. Zack worked with the girl at the Wendy's on Washtenaw Avenue, and he would never forget the look on her face when she found out what happened while she was working a shift at the drive-through. How did he go bad, everybody wondered, this son of a prominent realtor, pillar of the community? But Zack knew. The Demon Lord of Broken Concrete grew fat on his subjects' inchoate rage and pain. The survivors counted themselves lucky and wondered if they would be called upon either to provide a sacrifice or become one.

Love is a broken thing, is what Zack has learned. Broken like concrete, broken like a forgotten god. And you get up in the morning and they say they're sorry they slugged you, and you're just supposed to go on like it's all over even though the side of your face is swollen and it hurts to smile and everyone will try to be nice to you all day in a way that makes you want to die. That's the

Marquess of Daddy's Eighth Beer, or is it the Lord of I'll Give You Something to Cry About, reaching out through his father's hands to make himself known to Zack?

He swears he's never going to have children.

Because his car still isn't fixed, one night Zack sneaks out of the house to visit his girlfriend Mandy. After he's been there a while, the phone rings. She answers before her parents can get to it, covers for him. He's out the window before she hangs up, gets back to his house wide-eyed and sweaty, pretending he doesn't know anything about where he's been, like he was sleepwalking or something. His parents are uncertain, but JJ is genuinely frightened and that makes Zack feel shitty. The thrill of being out, giddy, it's all gone. He wants to tell JJ that he didn't mean it, just like he knows JJ didn't mean to hit him in the head with a piece of concrete on that sunny morning on the borderland between a subdivision and the surviving woods. The hard part about people caring for you is you're supposed to care for them back.

Time passes. Even after his parents have forgotten about it, even after JJ has forgotten about it, what stays with Zack is the moment when he and Mandy were lying on her bed, before the phone rang. What are you thinking about, she asked.

Air bubbling up from Tim's back. That's what he was thinking about, what he's thinking about now and always. The broken concrete boat ramp sloping away below his body into the brown water, where souls go, where gods wait.

■

Alex Irvine grew up mostly in Michigan and now lives in Maine. His fiction has won the Locus, Crawford, International Horror Guild, and Scribe awards. He once won a game of Jeopardy! and got Alex Trebek to bark. Cruise by alex-irvine.com to learn more.

POLAR SHIFT

--- ■ ---

Mir Seidel

Lev was outside, emptying the piss-pot in the snow, when the glow descended on him. He hurled the liquid in a high arc with the wind, away from the hut. The droplets crystallized into snow, fanning out in mid-air, just visible in the perpetual twilight.

The glow started before he'd lowered the pot—the cascade of snow shimmered as it fell, while the air around it stayed bright, then got even brighter, surrounding him with what looked like luminous bits of sand that made the thick flakes sparkle. It was everywhere. Lev breathed it in, felt it burrowing through his coat, sweaters, and long johns, through the pores of his skin. He couldn't catch his breath—he stumbled and fell, his body felt compressed like the snow under his knees. He couldn't help looking up into the veils of light rippling above him, gold with striations of blue and white, as the sound of pouring sand jingled all around.

Lev forced himself to his feet and shuffled in toward the hut, which was just a darker blur in the glow-cloud. He pulled the outer door open, then the inner one, without taking off his boots. He stood there stunned. Peering through tiny luminous whirlwinds, he saw Volya still at the table, making repairs to his headlamp.

"It's the glow," Lev said. "Do you feel it?"

Volya grunted. "Yeah. Made me drop a screw." The pieces laid out in neat rows around him.

Lev sat down on his bunk, his coat still on, feeling the glow as it swept through his body. He wanted to ask Volya if he'd ever been outside in a glow-storm, but forming words was too much effort. The waves of gold, crested with white and blue, buffeted through the room, more color than he'd seen in a year. More beautiful than anything he'd ever seen. As he slowly warmed up, the room returned to its usual gray-and-white, hard outlines. He stood and hung his coat over the heater. They were on their last main battery, running the heat just an hour at a time. The snow-treader was due soon—Efe would come, bringing them new batteries and food supplies.

What time was it? Lev had trouble considering this question, as if sand had blown into the gears of his internal clock, too. The calendar-clock told him it was almost 18 hours, the 21st of the month, and 87 days into the supply cycle. He slid the shutter back to look out the window. Watching the dim blue-gray still rippling with waves of glittering sand that lit up the snow, his heart entered his throat.

Volya pulled a frozen shad up from the food-hole for supper and split it down the belly. Lev went to the keyboard and unlocked the data safe.

"When did it start?" he asked. Volya looked at the clock. "Fourteen point four?" Lev typed in the time and other data. He'd lost several hours.

"I don't feel right," he said. He wasn't even hungry. "We can go out tomorrow."

He woke up and knew the storm had passed. But he felt on edge, not ready to trust the calm. The lamp was already on, and Volya had just come back inside with a pot of snow for coffee and washing. He shrugged off his coat and pulled off his snow-hood. His hair sprang out with static, the black mixed with gray. Looking at his deep-set frown and heavy eyebrows, Lev was hit with that strong sense of double familiarity, like déjà-vu but different: that he'd known Volya before. This could not be true. They had grown up in different cities, Lev in Shungdu in Novy Siberia, and Volya in Samara, from the Ural Group. Lev had been posted with the settlement forces for the Treaty Union, serving in Amazonia, while Volya had served in the border wars of Greater Thailand. They hadn't met before they were accepted for this assignment, with its extra pay and promise of a fat full-tour bonus.

He'd had this feeling before, and it gripped him tight, like always. Volya looked back at him, eyes wary in his stolid face.

"I knew you before this, didn't I?" Lev's throat was dry.

The other man closed his eyes, thinking, then shook his head. "I don't know."

The uncertainty of his answer added to Lev's edginess. They ate—he wolfed down the cold shad from last night, and Volya heated a chunk of cooked rice. Then they gathered up the magnetometer and other equipment and went out. Whenever a glow-storm receded, they had to go and check for a shift in the location of the magnetic pole. This was their job: recording the glow-storms' frequency and duration and marking the spot where the pole had traveled after the storm.

Lev had heard stories that the glow had been caused by some unknown material dropped from air-machines long ago, by ancient people trying to keep the ice from melting. If it was true, he guessed it must have succeeded. Or maybe they meant to melt the ice; either one sounded far-fetched to him. But the glow-storms never went away—at least up here, far from the hot zone and the nearest habitable zones.

The snow had drifted overnight, then hardened. No wind. They crunched forward in the half-dark without talking, pulling the sledge with the equipment. Under the black starry sky, Lev felt the particles stirring inside him, goading him. He glanced down at himself, feeling he might be glowing under his outdoor gear.

Finally, the Treaty Union flag showed in their headlamps. Bright red against white, frozen in place, twisted around its metal staff. The magnetometer stayed silent—that meant the Pole had moved somewhere else. This almost always happened in the storm's aftermath.

They leaned in to pull up the flagpole. Volya's snow-hood, lit by Lev's headlamp, quivered with golden sprays of light. *Dodging through streets he doesn't recognize, three or four boys around him. His foot slides on the wet pavement, he rights himself and keeps running. Panic, exhilaration.* They had already wrenched the staff out. Lev must have backed away. *A soldier behind, ordering them to stop. Heavy low clouds. A shot.* Volya, holding the flagstaff straight, stared at Lev.

"Did we run with the same gang?" Lev blurted.

"No," Volya said after a moment, shaking his head. Lev struggled to catch his breath, caught between running and standing still. Then he hefted the magnetometer and clomped a careful circle around Volya, still holding the flagpole, till they picked up a faint beeping in the still air. They trudged in that direction for twenty paces, then stopped so Lev could check the signal and adjust their direction. As they worked, glow-particles fell around them, making thin flurries in the still air. They repeated the process till the beeps turned into a continuous line of sound: they'd reached the new Pole.

They each bore down on the two-handled electric awl to drill the new hole. Together they set the flagpole in its new spot. The storm had moved the pole about a mile this time—a big jump. It might not make any difference. Or it might. The habitable-zone regions had agreed to abide by the longitudes set by the Treaty Union for legal disputes, fishing rights, that kind of thing. Up here, they wouldn't know whether the latest change mattered at all, at least not till the snow-treader came again with its months-old news.

Back at the hut, Lev sat at the keyboard to transcribe the readings from the magnetometer tracing the direction and distance to the new pole. He printed it out and sealed it in the rubber packing tube, along with a photograph of the calendar-clock.

The particles still moved inside him. They corkscrewed through his organs and bones, making their own spiraling arteries. Lev could barely sit through supper. Only watching Volya helped to anchor him: the long face, the close-spaced eyes with the vertical furrow between them. His frown as he chewed on the shad. The big hands handling the fork and knife with the same gentle firmness as when Volya was putting the headlamp back together.

After supper, they pulled out the baduk board and set up for a game. As they played, Lev had to squint to make out the pattern of his stones through sandy drifts.

Entering the interrogation room. Speaking to the prisoner—he's already confessed, can hardly hold his head up. Barking out the list of the prisoner's betrayals of the territorial government.

Volya stared at the stones on the board, not noticing as Lev struggled to breathe. Lev couldn't choose what came to him. He had to know.

"Did I ... shoot you?" He didn't say *kill*.

Volya looked up at Lev, his eyes unfocused. He turned his gaze back to the board. "I don't think so." He moved a piece.

Lev finally let out a long breath. He shook his head, willing away what he had seen, coming back into his body and the room lit by the cool white glow of the single lamp.

Volya opened the battery cabinet and checked the meter—it was down to its last tenth of ampere-hours. They had to cut back the stove to two hours a day, one in the morning and one at night. And they switched to candles, leaving the headlamps in reserve for going outside. Volya bent close to the candlelight to darn the socks, and Lev leaned in to fill in the daily log, and to recheck the med kit.

When he woke in the morning, Lev again felt the dryness of the sandy glow-particles wearing through him. He went out to empty the piss-pot and gather snow to melt on the stove. Stars winked above him; the lifting of polar night was still months away. Inside, he set the bucket on the stove. With only an hour of heat, the snow would melt and warm up, but not to boiling.

Breakfast was lukewarm instant coffee and oatmeal. Volya sipped and chewed. The sandy stuff whirled inside Lev, pushing him off balance.

Gray light coming through the kitchen window. A man sitting at the table, the newspaper open. A robe of shiny material spreads over the bulk of his well-fed body. Walking over, setting down two platters—a casserole, a mix of vegetables and meat he doesn't recognize, and another with rice. The scent of oil and unfamiliar spices warms him deep in his chest.

Volya was looking at him.

"Were you ... were we married?" Lev couldn't hold the words back. Being married was no more impossible than knowing each other some other way. Volya stopped chewing and his look went from wondering to thoughtful.

"No," he said finally. "That's not it." Lev sagged back in his chair, staring at the tepid oatmeal. Volya hadn't ridiculed him and hadn't taken offense. He'd considered the question seriously, as if trying it on. Which was good, because Lev had to know, and he needed Volya to tell him if the memory, or whatever, was right or wrong.

Volya went out after breakfast and didn't come back for a while. Lev knew he was looking for signs of the snowtreader. He returned hours later. Lips drawn tight, puffing out white nose-breaths, he hung his coat and snow pants over the stove to dry.

That night they started sleeping in Lev's bunk, arms around each other in their long johns. As the room grew colder and then went below freezing, Lev welcomed Volya's breath on his face, even with its smell of shad and coffee. The warmth of their bodies seemed to calm the sandiness inside him, at least while they lay there together.

They began sleeping longer each day, then not waking till afternoon. As the cold pressed in, it got harder to move, to get dressed, to go out and shovel snow and lift it into the bucket. After they ate, Lev would make a one-sentence entry in the daily log, then burrow back under the fur covers. Volya wiped off the dishes and utensils, examining each one before putting it away. One day, Lev couldn't get up for the second snow run. Volya went by himself and stayed out longer than he needed to again. When he came back, he sat down at the table, his coat and snow-hood still on, and didn't move.

"He's late," Lev said, meaning Efe. "But he'll get here." Volya didn't answer.

Lev made supper but Volya didn't eat, just sat staring at the calendar-clock.

The next day it was Volya who didn't get up. Outside, the wind shrieked.

Maybe Efe wasn't going to come. But if he did make it, they both had to be alive and working. Otherwise Volya would be replaced, and then he wouldn't get the full-tour bonus. Volya was sending all his pay to his sister in Nova Lisbon, to help her buy the unit she lived in. Then he would move in with her at the end of his tour. Lev had no plan like that—his pay just went right into his army account.

The guy Lev had replaced, Tran, hadn't finished his tour. Volya never talked about him, but Efe had said Tran had gone off the deep end. Could that be what was happening to Lev? The glow-storm had entered him, confusing him with these other lives that felt more real than this place? Maybe he and Volya were both losing it.

His skin prickling cold with fear, he shouted at Volya that he had to get up. Finally, he pulled Volya upright. He set his feet on the floor and worked his arms into his sweater. Too late for breakfast now, and they'd save the battery if they just had one meal. Lev pulled his coat down from where it hung over the stove. It was flecked with streaks of ice—the stove's heat had failed to dry it, and then it froze. He struggled into it, ice shards cracking away.

When he came back inside with the bucket of snow, Volya hadn't moved. Lev pulled the fur blanket up around Volya's shoulders. He made an early supper—barely defrosted shad and cubes of cold teff—and dragged the table over to the cot, but Volya didn't eat. He didn't look at the baduk board when Lev set it up. Lev played for both of them, commenting on each move. He ended the game, shivering, then climbed into bed and burrowed into the cave of fur blankets with Volya.

He woke up, sweating under the furs. His closed eyelids showed a field of dancing gold. The sand whipped through him with that high jingling sound.

Walking a dirt path through bushes. Bright sun, heat heavy in the air. Following someone: a woman, dressed in a kind of wrap, a cloth with many colors overlapping. He is small, she much bigger than him. The heat is like he's never known, brightness all around.

Lev forced his eyes open, weeping from the brightness. *They're at a market, setting out vegetables on the cloth she carried them in. He places them carefully, following the woman's movements. Is he a girl? The woman, his mother, sits down slowly—she is very pregnant. She banters and argues with people who stand over them. Everyone dressed in bright colors, shirts with no sleeves over shorts, or robes or wraps. Many people carrying small boxes in their hands that give out sounds of music and voices. Warm all around him, part from the heat, part from the enveloping feeling of knowing he belongs with these people, and this woman.*

Volya was talking in his sleep, half-formed words Lev couldn't follow, as if dreaming. Lev pulled him closer, tried to soothe him.

He lay there for a while, then hiked himself up on one arm, and looked until he could make out the calendar-clock in the receding glow. What day was it? How long since they'd gotten up from the bed?

Volya opened his eyes.

"We were someplace really hot," Lev whispered, sure now. "In the same family." He didn't say, *You were my mother.*

Volya took in a long breath, exhaled. "Yes."

Lev's head rolled back in relief. He lay on his back for a long time, taking in the feeling. When he curled back into Volya's arms, the man was already asleep and muttering more half-words. *They're sitting inside a small house made of earth. It feels like an oven, but not as hot as outside under the sun. His mother is slim again, and his baby brother squats nearby, drooling. The woman is arguing with a man who looms over them—his father? They're fighting about whether to stay or leave their home.*

They're walking on a dirt road, packed with people all moving in the same direction. Heat, bright-patterned clothes covered with brown dust. He is tired, so tired, asleep but still walking, then falling down. Mother holding him by the shoulders: Get up. You have to walk. She's carrying the baby and all the things they took, a pot, some clothes. They walk on and on. He thinks of just one thing—keeping her in his sight.

A loud banging. A voice yelling, cursing, calling their names. Lev scrabbled across the floor on all fours, lunging to open the inner door, then the outer one.

Efe stood there, his eyes wide. "What the hell— you look terrible, man." Lev's hand on the door looked grayish-brown, taut and bony. He started shaking and fell to his knees. Efe helped him over to the table, where he sat down heavy in the chair.

"What day is it?" His voice came out a hoarse whisper.

"Sorry I'm late, man. Paperwork's got worse, they wouldn't let me go." Efe moved easily into the room. With the snow-hood off, his face looked shiny and well-fed. Lev checked the calendar clock. It was day 113 of the supply cycle—Efe was almost three weeks late. Lev couldn't figure out how long they had been lying in bed. The sand inside him had receded, he realized, leaving empty channels behind.

"How's he doing?" Efe asked, nodding toward the bed.

"He'll be fine," Lev managed. "Just needs some hot coffee."

"It's fucking freezing in here. Help me get the stuff inside."

Efe had to do the hard work of lifting and carrying, since Lev could barely walk. Together they worked the new main battery into place. As the room rose above freezing, Efe made coffee, and Lev got Volya out of bed and walked him around. At the table, Lev washed Volya's arms and bare chest with warm water, marveling at his skin and the shiny scars on it, the whorl of hair just above his sternum. He was alive. They were both still here.

Seeing the shape they were in, Efe agreed to stay overnight. He went out to feed the two yaks that had followed behind the treader. At supper, he broke out a bottle that he'd brought as a peace offering.

"You guys are demented, staying up here like this," he teased. Volya gave a little half-smile that made Lev's heart jump. Efe was so loud and cheerful. He didn't know what happened here—no one else knew. Whoever was in charge thought that just the cold and the silence made it hard to stay up here. But Lev didn't want to leave. He wished Efe would go away, leaving just the two of them again, surrounded by darkness, finding their way in the world that kept growing between them. Even before they finished the bottle, Lev felt sick to his stomach and went to lie down. Efe took Volya's bunk.

His mother lies on the side of the road. She's weak with hunger, they all are. He sits beside her, fanning her with a big leaf. She has to be able to get up and keep walking. The baby stands between the mother's legs, fussing softly.

The next day, they packed up the hut. Lev felt—what? Tired and weak, strangely empty, and a kind of rightness to things as they put their blankets and smaller things in baskets and stuffed them in the vehicle's storage compartment. The sky was dead black, no hint of stars. Their headlamps lit the drifts of snow half-covering the yaks and the sledges. They moved the heater and the new battery out onto the sledges along with the furniture. Finally, they unscrewed the stakes at the hut's corners and hooked the structure to the tractor-harness.

Lev and Volya climbed into the cab with Efe. They started up the snow-treader and the yaks followed. The vehicle's heavy treads crushed the snow-dunes flat. Around them, steep walls of snow sparkled in its headlights. Every few minutes they stopped and Lev got out with the magnetometer to make sure they were on course to the pole.

The little flag still curled frozen around its staff. Efe got out, hooked the yaks up to the harness, and got the animals to maneuver the hut to a flat spot. The next time the Pole moved, at least they wouldn't have to go far to retrieve the flag and its staff. They staked the hut and then moved everything back inside.

Before Efe left, they all lined up under the calendar clock for a picture—proof that the two of them were still alive and able to carry out their duties. Volya was able to stand on his own. Efe elbowed them both and made a joke before the camera mechanism tripped—he wanted them to be smiling. The flash blinded him, but the pinpricks of light, so much like the sandy storm-particles, faded quickly. Efe added the picture to the rubber packing tube. They hugged him goodbye, even though he'd been late and they could have died.

Lev woke up, feeling unsettled. For a moment he didn't know where he was. Inside him, the sandiness stirred. A glow-storm must have happened in the night—he'd slept through it.

He sat up and slipped his feet into his indoor boots. The room was deliciously warm.

Volya stood there, looking at him, puzzled.

"We knew each other before, I think."

Lev was going to say *No, that couldn't be.* They'd grown up in two different cities and worked on different continents before they came here. But he felt an itch, an insistent sense of familiarity, like a halo of leftover glow particles binding them together.

Lev closed his eyes and nodded.

"I think so."

∎

Mir Seidel's novel, The Speed of Clouds *(New Door Books, as Miriam Seidel), explores the intersection of fandom and fantasy. Her short fiction and essays have appeared in* Into the Ruins, *the anthology* Breathe, *the* New York Review of Science Fiction, *and* Calyx *(forthcoming). She wrote the libretto for* Violet Fire, *about Nikola Tesla, which was performed in Belgrade, Serbia, and New York. She's also written about the arts for the* Philadelphia Inquirer, Art in America, *and other publications. She blogs at miriamseidel.com and tweets as Mir_QueenofMars.*

BACHELARD FORGETS THE KITCHEN

■

Cedrick May

He grunted, "It was only a dream ..." before rolling over again. But that is a string of nonsense words that carry no significant meaning, especially when the dream in question is the kind you can't find a way out of. And why in the world would anyone imply that a dream—*any* dream—could be harmless? Madness can come out of our dream-induced traumas, especially when we fail to master knowing our dreams from our waking hours ... Or does that even matter?

Jorge Louis Borges once wrote that dreaming and wakefulness were the pages of a single book, and that to live was to read the book one page at a time from cover to cover, but to dream was to skip through the pages at random. What a luxury it must be to choose which pages to land on. To know where you should slide your thumb on the dappled edge of the tome, to pick the very location you'll turn the stack of pages to in this brick of a book we call life. The opening? The middle? Straight to the finale in order to satisfy that unbearable curiosity to know the protagonist's (my own?) fate? If only I could read the spine of my own book, to see if my story is a drama, a fantasy, or even whether it's non-fiction at all! What category does the publisher of my tale place in tiny letters at the bottom of the back cover, right near the ISBN number, so that store clerks know where to place me on the shelves? What a pleasure it would be just to know the title—I might even have a name other than the one given to me by these strange people I find in my life.

He keeps calling me Janie, but am I *really* an Anne, a Tess, a Lizzie or possibly even a Tiffany?

I'm certainly no Lolita.

I think I may be a Carrie.

And I think Borges is right. Dreaming or awake, this thing I'm enduring must belong to the pages of some terrible, never-ending doorstop of a book that I have to master, or at least find some measure of control over.

But am I its author? Who is in control of this narrative? Borges never specified that ...

The man lying next to me is perturbed, I can tell that from his jerking and bouncing as he grumbles about my whining, taking too much cover as he rolls to face away from me in his cocoon of winter comforter, leaving me perched at the very edge of "my side" of the bed where the moving air chills me as it slides under the part of the comforter that doesn't quite fully cover me. Somehow, I know not to pull back any of the blanket he took from me, to disturb him now that *he* is comfortably warm and cozy, and I'm no longer screaming in my sleep.

This feeling of caution perplexes me.

I want to kill him.

I flip through the pages of my consciousness, trying to find the title page, or even the frontmatter, thinking they may have a clue as to the title or genre I'm working with here. If I'm going to kill the man lying next to me, knowing the genre will help me do it right.

I clearly land short of my goal, as I find myself in the seating area of an airport coffee shop. I have no idea why I am here, but I'm wearing sunshades and there's a throbbing pain in my jaw. There's a woman sitting across from me, thirtyish, broad-shouldered, well put together, actually quite elegant in a sort of chic, European way. She takes one of my hands in both of hers. She has a strong grip.

"You know you can stay as long as you want," she says to me, "Just tell me what you need." I remember her name is Stephanie.

"Do you have a compact, Steph?" I think I've always called her *Steph*. I try it out, even though it is an unnecessary narrative tag, in order to see her reaction. She doesn't bat an eye, so I think calling her *Steph* is normal.

Steph reaches into her purse and takes out a small round compact and hands it to me.

I open the compact and look into the mirror as I take the sunglasses off.

Instead of the black eyes and bruises I was expecting, I saw puffy, red-rimmed eyes that looked like I had been crying.

"Are you okay, honey?"

Steph's question barely registered in my mind as I studied my face, the dark, smooth features of a woman in her early thirties, cocoa brown and without a blemish.

Not one. Just the watery eyes of sadness and profound disappointment.

"Janie ...?"

So, it *is* Janie.

I close the compact and slide it across the table to my old friend just as a shadow crosses the table.

"I'm sorry for the wait, the staff here isn't very efficient ..."

I was startled by the basso voice of the man who was suddenly standing next to our table holding a cardboard tray of paper coffee cups and pastries. Steph patted my hand and gave me a concerned look, as if to say, *relax, it's okay* ... She turned and smiled up at the man, taking the tray and then rubbing his quite impressive arm as he sat down next to her. He and Steph kissed and that was when I remembered they were married—Steph and Dieter.

They seem so happy.

I've known Steph since high school, and I recalled how she used to brag about how she liked her men like she liked her coffee—black! She would laugh and laugh at this, but she was serious. I didn't date much, but I took whatever I could get when I could get it. Steph, on the other hand, dated a *lot*, and always black men, all the way through to our senior year in college. Until Dieter.

We had gone to this little dive jazz bar about four miles from campus at the corner of Division and Bowen Avenue. We'd never heard of it before, but someone we knew told us about it and since we were bored decided to go.

The place was a mess. Looked like a half-dressed barn on the inside, and we were the only black people out of about a dozen patrons and the two-person staff there—including the band! Dieter was the lead guitar player, and after the band's second set, he hopped off the stage and just strode over to our table and started talking to Steph in that deep, smooth German accent of his. He was polite to me, too, but he was clearly there for Steph.

I watched as Miss Black Coffee practically wet herself sitting there, stumbling over her words, and giggling like we were back in high school.

I had to finish college practically by myself, because those two became inseparable. I remember being happy for Steph, but I had to jibe her about her change in beverages.

"I thought you like black coffee? Guess you've switched to cream, huh?" I laughed.

"Yes, girl, and it sure is *sweet*!"

Steph and Dieter sat across the table from me now, looking at me with concern and pity. But pity for what, exactly? What's my story?

"We should have had you come stay with us here a long time ago, anyway," Dieter said, "The fall is beautiful this time of year, and next week we can take the train to the Oktoberfest down in Munich."

Is this dream just an adult drama? Is it all about me leaving my—well, whomever that is in my bed later in this story—leaving that man to come for a visit with my friends in Frankfurt? I look across the table at Steph and Dieter smiling and whispering to each other in German. Steph seems particularly giddy. Maybe they're planning to introduce me to a big hunky German man like Dieter, maybe this is a *Romance*. Maybe that's what I need.

But my heart isn't in that.

I try to use telepathic powers to make Steph and Dieter's hair catch on fire. They just continue to sip on their coffee and make plans for my visit.

I'm thinking about the man lying next to me in bed a few chapters ahead, and I take out my cellphone to see if I can pull up photos of him. I have questions that need answers, and if I can't set Steph and Dieter on fire (since this is apparently not a horror novel I'm flipping through), then at least they can give me some answers.

The problem is, I don't have any pictures of the man lying in bed next to me. All of the pictures are of me and some other man I don't recognize.

All of the pictures.

I don't know exactly why, but my heart begins to beat hard against my chest and my throat feels full. I stop swiping when I land on a picture of the man and me standing shoulder to shoulder, smiling. We appear to be at a party, we look happy. I hold the cellphone up to Steph and Dieter.

"Who is this?" I say a little too loud. My hands are shaking.

Steph and Dieter look at the photo, and then at each other, and then back at me. There is confusion on their faces. Steph puts her coffee down and places a calming hand on the table between the two of us.

"Honey," she says in a voice so quiet it is barely audible, "You know who that is. That's your ex-husband."

Tears come to my eyes, and I feel like puking. I don't know the man in the picture.

"Then who is the man lying in my bed with me?" I say this a little too loud again. People at the next table look over at us. I wish I could make their hair catch on fire. This isn't a *romance*—I won't let it be ...

"*Who am I lying next to in bed?*" I yell, this time as I shove the cellphone photo toward their faces. Steph can't talk, she starts to cry.

"We should leave now, go to the house for a talk ..." Dieter says, standing, placing a hand on Steph's back and elbow to help her up.

"*Who am I ...*" I begin to stand, too, still holding the phone out at my friends, knowing that what I'm doing isn't very kind or generous, but I don't care—I don't care for the kind of story they're trying to lead me into—I have to take back control ...

But as I stand, my head begins to spin, and I find myself falling backward—white, dappled pages flip across my vision like the pale wings of flocking birds startled from a restful reverie ...

I'm lying back again in the bed next to the man who has rolled once more in the covers, having taken even more from me while I was gone. There's barely a flap of comforter left covering me, and I am cold.

I slide from under what's left of my covers, careful not to shake the bed or bump the side table and shuffle out of the dark bedroom and into the hallway. I make my way to the kitchen.

As I step slow and careful through the darkness, I think about what Gaston Bachelard said about houses, that our homes shelter our dreams and protect the dreamer, that the home allows one to dream in peace.

I don't feel very peaceful here.

I just skipped across chapters like Borges said, and now I'm reading the pages of my walk from the bedroom to the kitchen in the dark, and I don't feel at ease at all, from either the dreaming or wakefulness. My feet seem to know the way, without any illumination, but the familiarity with the house's geography doesn't give me any solace.

Bachelard has never been in *my* house.

And while he talked a lot about attics and cellars, he never mentions the kitchen. How can a Freudian philosopher *not* talk about kitchens, for Christ's sake?

I stand in my own kitchen looking into the night through the wide, bay window. There's a waxing, gibbous moon bright enough to let me see the details of a well-manicured, but empty, back yard. I turn, and the silver light coming through the window (and my eyes already having adjusted to the darkness) allows me to find my way through the bare kitchen to the silverware drawer where I take out a butcher knife.

I find my way back to the bedroom and slide back under what's left of the covers not wrapped around the man with his back to me. His head pokes out from the comforter cocoon he's wrapped himself in and I start to wonder ...

How should I do this?

This surely wasn't a part of the dream *we* had planned to share, right?

His neck and body are wrapped too protectively inside his comforter cocoon, so I place the point of the butcher knife right below the base of his skull, in the little crevasse where the back of the head ends and the top of the spine begins. Just inside that little indentation. The same kind of spot I might put the blade when carving between the bones of a turkey leg at Thanksgiving, or the meat between the hard bones on a rack of spareribs. I know this knife will slide in there easily, right through his spinal cord and into the brain. I've practiced this many times before while preparing dinner.

I get ready to push, but the pages flip with a sudden white fluttering and I find myself spinning backward again through the narrative. I reach out to grab the bedpost, to stop myself from falling away from this crucial moment, but my fingers slip on something wet and slippery, and I spin through the flurry of whiteness, unable to hang on to this moment. I open my mouth to scream, but nothing comes out but a long, hollow breath.

...

I'm standing in darkness, again. Can barely see. I raise my hand and feel a wall just a foot or so in front of me. There's something on my hand, too. It's wet. I realize the wetness is sticky, too. I'm still holding the butcher knife in my other hand.

I hear a sucking sound.

No, more like gurgling.

Behind me.

I turn and my breath catches in my throat. In the light of the moon coming through the window, I see them. Two baby cribs, side by side. I know what's inside them.

My dream. Somebody's dream.

I can't breathe.

I need to get away. I fall forward quickly, jumping to a new chapter only to find myself trapped, unable to move. I'm in a blinding white room and I feel like I'm strapped down. I yank at my restraints, but they refuse to give.

I scream.

"Help me! *Somebody, help me!*"

...

The pages turn quickly. In fact, I skip farther back than ever before, leaping over a huge chunk of the narrative in one big turn of pages.

I'm at the party now. The one from the cellphone. In the airport. I'm with the man in the picture I showed to Steph and Dieter. We're smiling big for the picture, but I don't feel happy. The woman who takes the picture hands me my phone with a smile. I thank her and look at the photo as she turns to go. The man in the picture, whatever his name is, doesn't have a genuine smile. It's totally fake. So's mine. I didn't see it in the airport, but I see it now.

I turn to say something, but he's already walked away, heading for the front door.

I think we've had an argument.

It's an old argument.

Flip ...

The wedding is beautiful, and everyone is smiling. Great big champagne grins and singing. The man lying next to me in bed is in a tuxedo now, lifting me in his arms. My chest is full of joy, about to burst wide open as we embrace once more, kissing deeply.

He smells so good. I feel like I'm about to fly away.

I know it won't last, tough. I've already flipped too far ahead—or is the man lying next to me in bed somewhere in the *past*, some earlier moment in the pages of this book?

Oh, how I wish that would be the case now—I want *this* moment to last forever!

But now I'm back in the dark room looking at the two baby cribs. I know what's inside them. I just know.

Somebody else's dream that would not be denied.

I walk with slow, heavy steps to the side of the cribs and look inside.

There they are, in the silver light of the gibbous moon, sleeping. My twins. My two babies. One of them is gurgling wet snores through his wide-open mouth.

The other child stirs.

It's about time for them to feed again, so I put the butcher knife on the changing table and pick up the waking child before he can disturb Mr. Snores. I sit in the comfy rocking chair in the corner and lift my blouse over my left breast so the baby can find it. Even in his half-awake state, he finds the nipple and latches on, feeding in his sleep as if it were his last supper.

I stroke the child's bare head and soft cheeks. The wet stickiness on my hand smears over him, and I can see it matting his hair and glistening over his skin in the silver light coming through the window.

I feel out of breath as the man in bed next to me shakes me awake.

"Holy shit, Janie," he says, "You were screaming again."

"I'm sorry."

"Maybe don't eat so close to bedtime anymore, okay?"

"It was horrible. I was ..."

"It was only a dream, Janie. Get some sleep now." The man turns away again to lay on his side, facing the opposite wall. He's fast asleep in no time and I'm just lying there thinking about the babies and all of the blood.

What would Borges say about this? Symbolism? Allegory? No, he's not a Freudian like Bachelard. Borges was a poet. He would say there is no difference between dreaming and wakefulness. He would say both are a part of life.

I carefully slide from beneath the covers left over by the man lying next to me. There is something I need to get from the kitchen.

■

Cedrick May lives in the Dallas/Fort Worth area where he teaches African-American literature and screenwriting at The University of Texas at Arlington. Cedrick has stories published or forthcoming in Aphelion, Coffin Bell, Dark Horses Magazine, Road Kill: Texas Horror by Texas Writers, Volume 7, *and* Violent Delights & Midsummer Dreams: A Gothic Anthology of Shakespeare Retellings.

STRANGE EONS

■

Keira Perkins

The elder gods arrived in the sky in early September, like an unholy aurora borealis stretching across a midnight sky. Their vastness blocked the sun, an unending eclipse, a liminal state, a breath that was inhaled but never let go. Lovecraft got it wrong, I think. It was not the sight of the gods that made humanity go mad. It's what they destroy that hurts us. Somehow, these elder gods, these aliens, had killed time itself.

Since their arrival, I have been taking refuge in the cornfields. If I stare at the aliens too long, my head aches and my stomach twists, like I'm crashing from a sugar high. I feel a little better when I sit in the dirt and look up at the stalks above me. Since time died, the leaves and stalks no longer sway because there is no longer wind. It's okay though. Mostly. I don't miss the wind that much. I like how the corn reaches towards the sky, toward the gods, like Adam's outstretched arm in the Sistine chapel. Something about that eternal reach makes this infinite moment and those colossuses in the sky feel smaller in comparison.

"Not smaller," I say to myself and the corn, "just more manageable. Infinity is an absolute and it can't be smaller than it is."

I've spent a long while thinking about it. There's lots of people to talk to; everyone has an opinion on our new reality, after all. But the frenetic and sickening energy from other people is exhausting and I am barely hanging onto my sanity as it is. My thoughts have felt tangled and fuzzy lately, and other people's thoughts make that tangled feeling worse. It's another reason that I hide away in the corn. The corn is quiet, and I like to press my knees to my chest and dig my bare toes into the dirt. I am aware that I am literally grounding myself, but I don't care that it looks stupid. I can't remember the last time it rained, but deeper down, the soil is still wet. I like the coolness of it against my skin.

It should be an obvious conclusion that the soil is still wet. Evaporation, after all, takes place over time and time is dead. It should be as easy as that to learn the new rules of time's destruction, but it's not. Everything is strange and inconsistent in a way that makes normal, everyday things hard to predict and plan. It makes your thoughts tangled and fuzzy. There is no weather, but the worms still dig. There is no rain, but the corn still lives. There is no time, but the Earth still spins.

None of it makes sense, but I think maybe only linear time has stopped following the laws of thermodynamics. My theory is that the elder gods or aliens or whatever, are actually mostly made of dark matter. They're heavier than they should be, and their resultant dark gravity compresses everything all together, including time. It's like coal and diamonds. If you squish coal with enough weight, it eventually turns into a diamond, even though it's still made of the same stuff as coal. So, like, our time would have been squished hard and gotten us stuck here, forever frozen in some cosmic amber. It's still the same stuff as before, but it looks different. Non-linear time, if that exists, just kind of does whatever it feels like.

As much as I've tried to ignore everyone, I know this theory has occurred to other people. The rebuttal is that if dark gravity was that strong, the aliens would be a black hole that swallowed us up before we ever saw them. We would be squished flat and dead and possibly only two-dimensional. Or maybe not, is the rebuttal to that rebuttal. Time and energy and light bend near black holes, which would explain why time is a clusterfuck, but doesn't explain anything else. Some people think that time is actually *dead* dead, and we're in its rotting corpse. I don't like that theory.

The physicists have been shouting a lot and I've seen a few of them in tears on YouTube and TikTok while trying to explain time dilation and quantum mechanics. I feel bad for them because they seem to feel just as sick and tangled up about it as I do. I don't have room in my head for their bad feelings, too. I deleted all the social media apps off my phone, and I don't carry it anymore. I don't want to know what other people are thinking.

There are a few things about this new reality that I think are true. Life itself didn't stop when time did, even though everything else had. It wasn't obvious at first. But then children stopped hitting their developmental milestones. People in hospice care, like the ones that were literally taking their last breaths, still lived. Pregnant people stayed pregnant. Hair and nails stopped growing.

We all still need to breathe though, and I don't understand why, if I'm being honest. At first, I would hold my breath for as long as I could to test time. I would count, "one one thousand, two one thousand, three one thousand ..." in my head because no one's clocks, or watches, or phone timers were working anymore. I made it to two minutes and fifteen seconds, until I started gasping like a dying fish. It's just as well, I was seeing spots and it was making my head harder to live in.

We can all still eat, too, but no one's hungry. We can still drink, but no one's thirsty. I don't know how bodies can still consume if they aren't metabolizing, but I don't think about it too closely because, again, it makes my head hurt. Most of my family members are always drunk now, which shouldn't be possible if they aren't metabolizing the alcohol.

I'm careful these days, if it is "these days" and not "this day", to not get within their arms' reach. My grandma and my mom are always sloppily grabbing at me and pulling me close into tight hugs that last too long. I think they're making me claustrophobic. I feel trapped. My grandma hugs me the most, and the smell of the vodka on her breath overwhelms all my senses and pushes me to the verge of panic. It's the same smell that was often on my mother, even before the aliens had arrived, but at least she wasn't a hugger. They both thought I couldn't smell it, but I can. Even when they tried to hide it in their iced tea or their orange juice, I could smell it. Pregnancy had made my nose more sensitive.

"Do you know about MK-Ultra?" my grandmother likes to loudly whisper in my ear while stroking my back, "They've done this before. Those dirty sneaks"

"They think we belong to them, to use anyway they want." says my mother, her eyes flashing, "They always have."

I'm not sure what my mom's talking about. She may be right, but I don't think either of us know who "they" are. Grandma thinks the CIA has dosed the water supply with LSD. I think most theories are just as unlikely as another, but grandma's feels especially unlikely. Mass hallucinations exist, of course, but the CIA dosing 8 billion people simultaneously feels improbable. If the water in Flint still wasn't drinkable, how could that same government be able to impact the global supply of water? And not only that, make us believe that there were aliens in the sky that had completely stopped life as we knew it? Unless the government is just really good at gaslighting and poisoning water? I can feel my thoughts start to do that tangly thing again and I take a deep breath. As I exhale, I dig my toes deeper into the soil.

All of that doesn't answer the "why" of it all though. I think I know. I'm so afraid to say it outside my own head. I think I killed all of us, but the terrible thing is, I would do it again. The elder gods had arrived the evening after the morning I had an abortion. I've wondered many times if I had been carrying an antichrist. Not *The Antichrist*, but maybe a minor one. I don't think I'm important enough for the main event, you know? The aliens feel evil, or at least they make me feel really sick, which makes me think the embryo was something bad. It makes me feel so guilty. How could I have been growing something so bad in my own body?

I'm so afraid that they want their antichrist and now they're hunting me so the plan can be corrected. My stomach flips and twists and panicked bile rises in my throat when I imagine being pregnant again. I would do anything to get away. I can't get away. All I have is the cornfield, and I am so grateful that I'm essentially invisible when I sit at the base of the stalks. Maybe they can't see me down here. Just in case though, I dig my toes deeper into the soil. I'm hopeful it will anchor me more securely and keep me away from the aliens' eyes. I'm not sure they have eyes in those swirling, colored tentacles, but it hurts too much to study them too closely.

When the politicians and holy men had preached that natural disasters were brought about by an angry god and human sin, I doubt they had intended these gods. I really doubt that they had imagined me carrying a harbinger of death in my womb. I laughed until I made myself sick when I thought about it too much. I've mostly stopped thinking about it.

As I push my toes down, a cicada's head pushes its way through the soil near my big toe, grasping and pushing its way free. I scowl at it, hoping it takes the hint. It is not the right month for cicadas. It's not even the right cycle for this species. The ones with red eyes only emerge every seventeen years.

"Hey, little guy," I say, "This is the wrong time for you. Go back to sleep."

The cicada nymph does not agree. It continues to thrash, its small arms cutting like flippers through an ocean of dirt. I watch it quietly, fascinated as it fully emerges and begins its climb up my big toe. I don't like the feel of its feet. They remind me of fishhooks. I watch as the cicada continues its awkward march down my foot and towards my ankle, looking for higher ground for the final stage of its metamorphosis. I shudder, involuntarily, the sensation of its feet against my skin is too much. I usually like cicadas, but I don't want this one to crawl on me.

"Go molt somewhere else," I say, "Your feet feel like nails down a chalkboard."

Very gently, I pluck the cicada from my foot with my thumb and forefinger and place it on the nearest corn stalk. The cicada's legs swing wildly until they find purchase on the stalk and grasp it tightly. I watch it continue its ascent. I wish it had already discarded its shell; those cicadas will sing if you squeeze them very, very gently. This one can't sing yet.

"Do you think we're dead?" I ask the insect, "Maybe this is hell."

The cicada does not answer. I know I am slowly losing my mind, but at least I am not surprised when it doesn't reply.

I take my toes out of the dirt and sit cross-legged as I watch the cicada shed. The wings slowly start to emerge, but it takes a long while. I like to watch these moments occurring and progressing even though time itself is broken. Like I said, it doesn't make sense. Children have stopped growing but an insect can still molt? I'm deep in my own tangled thoughts when I hear something large fighting its way through the corn. It's silly to fight the field when the corn is this tall; you can never win. It's much smarter to follow the rows, which let you ride along them like a wave to shore. Besides, there are always small gaps in the stalks you can slip through if you are patient enough to find them. The corn near me begins to sway and then a face is visible through the stalks.

"Hey, Jaxon," I say.

"Hey!" My boyfriend trips over a root and crashes to the ground, bringing multiple plants down with him. Jaxon is not patient. I've told him many times about how to navigate the corn, but he still insists on doing it his way.

"Ow." Jaxon gingerly pushes himself up and sits back on his heels. He examines his palms carefully, which are scraped and slightly bleeding. His jeans are dirty at the knees, but not torn.

"You okay?" I ask. He seems mostly unhurt, but things are weird, and I don't want to assume. I flick my eyes to the cicada to make sure it's still safely anchored on its nearby stalk. I am relieved when I spot it.

Jaxon nods. "Yeah, your mom said I could find you out here. What are you doing out in the corn again?"

I shrug. It feels like a lot to explain.

"Are you bleeding? Oh, my God. Are you hurt?"

I follow Jaxon's eyesight to my thigh. I'm still sitting cross-legged. I had jumped back slightly when Jax fell, and I see my dress has hiked up high on my leg. It's smeared dark with brownish blood.

"Oh. That."

I'm not alarmed. It's only period blood, and I've been bleeding for quite some time, I think. It's hard to judge how long I've bled, but I know it started after I took the pills at the clinic. Sometimes the blood is bright red, sometimes there are dark maroon clots, but most days it's a sticky reddish-brown. Jaxon did have a point though. I've been bleeding steadily since time stopped. Or broke. Died. Whatever. And if reality were still real and time still passed, I should have bled out months ago. Everyone else I knew no longer had a period. No one else I knew was being hunted by the elder gods. None of this was fair at all.

"Why are you bleeding? Jesus!"

"Because I have a uterus, Jaxon. And it's shedding." I say this flatly. There is no use in getting upset about facts. Your mind gets all tangly when you don't accept facts, like how there are Lovecraftian nightmares hanging like a string of Christmas lights above us.

Jaxon is quiet for moment. I assume talking about my uterus shedding has made him think of the abortion. I think I'm right because he asks me suddenly, "Will you let me pray with you?"

"No." My voice is still flat. We've had this conversation before.

"We're being punished."

I roll my eyes at him. I'm not trying to be unkind, but he really is exasperating. I feel like I've aged a thousand years, and he still gets to be seventeen. Maybe time hasn't completely stopped for me after all. I'm suddenly exhausted, both with the weight of my age and weight of his immaturity. Lots of people have abortions and God or gods or aliens or whatever don't kill time because of it.

"We are! Look at the sky! Just look at it! What do you think that is if it's not God's punishment?" Jax starts the words at a shout but is whispering them by the end. He's nearly in tears.

I think it's a strange directive from him. Jaxon has been looking steadily at anything else but the sky since the aliens arrived. Even now, his eyes are fixed on my blood-smeared thigh as he gestures toward the elder gods. It's time for that to stop.

I place my hand under Jaxon's jaw, gently turn his chin upward and lean in, as if for a kiss. Instead, I point to the sky and say "Does that look like Jesus, Jaxon? Does it? Is it the Father, The Son, or The Holy Ghost? Does it look like any angels you've ever heard of? That mess of tentacles doesn't even look like a biblical one."

Jaxon trembles slightly, but to his credit, he doesn't look away. Electric purple tentacles are pulsating against a twilight sky. He says, "Maybe they're demons."

I snort. "No. They aren't demons." I consider some more and add, "I think they might be evil though. But like, an evil that exists, not a paranormal one."

Jax's eyebrows furrow. He doesn't understand my tangled thoughts and I don't blame him.

"I think they're demons," he says again.

"They aren't demons." We've had this argument before.

Neither of us speaks, until Jaxon blurts into the silence, like he's vomiting, "I would have loved you both."

We've argued about this too. I cup his face in my hands and say, "If you loved me, you would have protected me. You would have driven me to the clinic in Illinois and held my hand. You would have walked with me past those protesters as they called me a murderer. You would have held my hair back when I vomited. You would have paid for at least part of it, so I wasn't scrambling for cash. My sister did all of that. And if you loved me, like you say you do, my sister wouldn't want to kick your ass."

Jaxon stays silent. I've thought about this a lot though, and I'm tired of defending myself. I lightly slap his cheek, then again for emphasis, and his eyes fill with tears again. I'm not angry, and I know he's not hurt. I'm too tired to be angry and I need him to listen.

"Those aren't demons," I continue, "HP Lovecraft was a racist and giant weenie about most things, but he was a little bit right about the elder gods. They're just aliens or whatever that make you feel bad and crazy."

Jaxon is still silent. I sigh. It's going to take more for him to understand me. I feel cruel. I feel like a monster. I wonder if he thinks I am a monster.

"It doesn't matter that you would have loved us both." I tell him. "That wouldn't have paid our rent or bought us groceries. What were you going to do? Go off to college with your baseball scholarship and drink yourself stupid every weekend? Do I stay in this town I hate and work at Dollar General? Should my alcoholic mom and grandma babysit our kid? Would you come home to visit until it was no longer fun, and you found yourself a cool girl to fuck instead?"

Jaxon's eyes flash with anger and I think idly that he might hit me. That's fine. I've been fantasizing about breaking his nose and making him bleed; I just need an excuse. I don't know if it's the aliens' influence or if I'm a violent monster that was carrying an antichrist, and that's another thing I don't like to think about too much. All I know is that it's a terrible thing to love and hate someone in equal measure.

It's a long moment stuck in this broken moment, but neither of us hits the other. I point at the nearby cornstalk and say, "Jax. Do you see that cicada?"

He scowls at me. He thinks I'm attempting to change the subject, but he looks anyway. He says, "I hate when they look like that. Those giant wings poking through their shell as they bend backward is so creepy."

"That's a terrible thing to say about a baby."

The scowl deepens into a glare of disgust, still furious but now he's confused too.

"I was eight weeks pregnant. That *person* you're so concerned about was less formed than a cicada nymph. Smaller, too." I consider it some more and then add, "That cicada can live on its own and it's not bothering anyone. But if it needed your blood and bones to survive and its song got too loud, you'd kill it in a heartbeat. You wouldn't even flinch. You want it dead now because it's creepy"

Jaxon is listening, but his jaw is tight. I tell him, "Staying pregnant would have destroyed my life. So if I have to choose, I'm going to pick me. I'm allowed to pick me. You can grieve all you want, but don't you dare shame me for saving myself. You say you love me? Don't you dare act like I'm worthless."

Jax doesn't answer me. I know him well enough to know he doesn't agree. I wonder if he's thinking of when we snuck off from the bonfire last summer and into the cornfield with a blanket. I wonder if he regrets it. I think that getting pregnant as the broken stalks poked my back, as we fumbled with each other, awkward and inexperienced, had to be the elder gods attempting a cosmic joke. It feels like the evil shit they would do. My boyfriend, who says he loves me, doesn't understand the existential horror I felt when I was pregnant, and that feels like a joke too.

I breathe deeply, trying to re-ground myself. I am still bleeding. I hate it. I wonder how much of my blood has soaked down into the earth as I live this same time over and over. I wonder if the soil is wet from my blood and not the memory of rain. My head hurts. My head always hurts.

I see a bit of dirt near my foot jump like a stray popcorn kernel. One, then three, then five pops and suddenly the dirt is like a pot of water simmering. The simmering turns to a boil, that ripples and spreads like rings in a pond. Jaxon doesn't notice yet because he's staring at the sky, but I see more hard-shelled cicadas starting to poke through the dirt. They should still be sleeping. Why aren't they sleeping?

How long have we been stuck here in this broken and dead time that the cicadas are now awake? Why are the elder gods hanged and unmoving in the sky? What do they want? Why does everything feel so awful, and stagnant, and sick?

Suddenly, understanding hits me like a thunderclap and I laugh. I can't stop laughing and then I am howling and crying, and my stomach is cramping, and my nose is running, and I can't stop. I. Can't. Stop. My thoughts have become untangled, and this clear understanding is far, *far* worse. Jaxon has gripped my shoulders tight as he shakes me, and I know I will have finger-shaped bruises, but it doesn't hurt. He's shouting, his face contorted with fear, asking me what's wrong.

I can't tell him. Not at first. But I finally manage to gasp through my tears and chattering teeth, *"That is not dead which can eternal lie, and with strange eons even death may die."*

I hate Lovecraft, *so* much. He got almost everything wrong. Time is dead and gods are dead but not dead, and cicadas lie dormant for years and years and everything, simply *everything* is strange and wrong and those aren't *normal* cicadas. I point toward the dirt where the earth is rolling now like a wave, like a localized earthquake. A swarm of cicadas, hundreds and thousands and hundreds of thousands push their way up and out of the earth.

Crawling and skittering, they hook their feet into Jaxon's shoelaces and jeans. They are in my hair and on my face and I can feel their weird fishhook feet on my skin, and I am shuddering like the earth. They crawl up the stalks, higher and higher. Jaxon, the cornstalks, and I are covered in a blanket of insects. I cannot see us. I cannot see the corn. I only see their red eyes.

But then Jax's face turns toward me, and his beautiful hazel eyes are wide with fear, their light browns and greens screaming in contrast to the cicada's dark browns and blacks. He is so close to actually screaming, it's a wonder that he hasn't yet. I reach out to take his hand and squeeze it; begging him silently not to scream. I don't think it's a good idea to scream. I want to speak, but I am afraid of these strange insects crawling into my mouth, grasping my tongue and choking me. Jax seems to understand the look I give him. We sit as still as we can, holding hands and the cicadas molt, quicker than I've ever seen. Quicker than I thought they could. Their translucent purple wings emerging, bloodred bodies breaking free, and fluttering, and drying, and suddenly they are all singing, deafening us, and time around us has frozen, somehow, again, a moment trapped in a moment. We have always been in this swarm that blots out the sky, and we will always be.

Then an eon later that is just as sudden as the moment before, they take flight and rise high, a cloud that is heavy and fat on my blood. Higher and higher, they fly onwards, singing towards the gods in the sky. They are so high now that I can't hear them, but my ears still ring from their song. My skin still crawls from the feel of their feet. The elder gods' tentacles reach down and surround the cicadas like a cage and pull them close. I see other dark clouds on the horizon and more writhing tentacles reaching and scooping.

I feel the dried salt of my tears on my cheeks, as the wind blows across my face. It is finished. And I understand now. This wasn't a punishment, like Jax thought. They weren't hunting me to regain an antichrist, like I thought. They simply needed my blood, and I was an opportunity. Evil gods always need blood. Evil gods needed my confusion, and desperation, and my shame and my fear to feed and raise their legion that lay sleeping. They bled me dry of *myself* because I was nothing but a vessel for them. And now they have their swarm.

I am afraid of how many swarms they've raised.

I am afraid of what may come next.

The tentacles are retracting, slowly. I am afraid they will return. But for now, they are pulling away and the sunlight has begun to peek through. My thoughts are tangled again with hope and fear, and I am full of rage and fury. But for now, I am safe. For now, I am free. This moment is evil and blood-soaked, and it is finally time to leave.

■

Keira Perkins lives in Indiana with her husband, dogs, cats, and whichever stray animal she's brought home that week. When she's not writing, she gets paid to be a scientist. Keira can be found on Twitter as @hellaciousK and at keiraperkins.wordpress.com.

PARTIAL TRANSCRIPT FROM THE GREAT BREXIT BAKING SHOW
SEASON 23, EPISODE 4

─────────── ■ ───────────

Rich Larson

```
EXT. LAWN - DAY

Drone's eye view of massive rectangular
white TENT centered on verdant lawn.
Gleaming metallic GARDENING BOTS trundle
across the grass, snipping and spritzing.

Cheery music plays as we zoom in on the
show's HOST, EDDIE TART, standing outside
the TENT. He is a sallow, sweaty man in a
floral-printed suit.

                EDDIE TART
     Welcome, welcome, one and all,
     to our twenty-third season! Once
```

>   again, we've scoured the isle to
>   find the very best amateur bakers
>   in England -- and by extension,
>   the world -- for a gruelling,
>   six-week competition that will
>   put their skills to the test! And
>   this week? Things are going to
>   get chocolatey!

Zoom out as EDDIE TART beams and waves. Aerial view of the CONTESTANTS walking in single file toward the TENT, most carrying parasols for shade. The drone rises slightly too high: on the borders of the lush green lawn, we see withered yellow grass and desiccated dirt.

INT. TENT - DAY

Interview shot of CONTESTANT with caption: SANDRA, 37, GUILDFORD. She has darting dark eyes and a nervous smile.

>   SANDRA
>   I've honestly never worked
>   much with chocolate, as, you
>   know, it's quite expensive, and
>   obviously the synthetic cocoa,
>   that Brit Bar stuff, is just --

> She blinks rapidly.

It's great, and the fact that
it's manufactured here in
England, well, that makes it
taste all the better! Doesn't it?

Interview shot of CONTESTANT with caption:
JOHN, 44, LIVERPOOL. He has thick glasses,
sparse gray hair, a shell-shocked gaze.

> JOHN
> It's going to be a disaster. I
> mean, it's bloody 54 degrees
> Celsius today. I just don't
> understand why they keep doing
> this, why every year they act as
> if --

EXT. JUDGES' GAZEBO - DAY

A small climate-controlled pagoda with
tinted glass windows.

> EDDIE TART (V.O.)
> *It's an unseasonably warm summer
> this year, and you have to wonder
> if the heat might be a factor for
> our brave chocolatiers! Let's
> get the scoop from our judges,*

> *renowned pastry chef DIANA DALTON*
> *and simulated legacy intelligence*
> *PAUL HOLOGRAM!*

INT. JUDGES' GAZEBO - DAY

DIANA DALTON, wearing a thoughtful smile and a navy pantsuit patterned with tiny Union Jacks, is seated on a sleek white couch. PAUL HOLOGRAM, a heavy-set old man with a neatly trimmed beard and bright blue eyes, sits beside her. There are occasional flickers of pixelation when he moves.

> DIANA DALTON
> Oh, it's certainly going to be a challenge for them. I advocated for a sealed kitchen with proper climate control, but Paul here always gets his way, don't you, Paul?

> PAUL HOLOGRAM
> During my career I've baked in all sorts of conditions, Diana. It never killed me.

> DIANA DALTON
> What did kill you, Paul?

PARTIAL TRANSCRIPT FROM THE GREAT BREXIT BAKING SHOW

                PAUL HOLOGRAM
                  (chuckling)
Bit of a personal question, there, Diana. Tell you one thing: it wasn't melted chocolate.

                DIANA DALTON
What a wonderful way to go that would be! Let me just toddle off to have my neural patterns uploaded, then -- then come back and drown myself in a vat of dark chocolate.

    She gives a pained smile.

Delicious.

INT. TENT - DAY

Two rows of countertops and ovens fill the space, with pop-up pantries and freezers at the back. Frenzied activity as the CONTESTANTS race against time, whisking egg whites, rolling out rough puff, sectioning thick slabs of chocolate. They are drenched in sweat.

EDDIE TART, DIANA DALTON, and a clicking rolling spheroid wander the tent,

observing the various creations underway.
They stop at JOHN's countertop.

> DIANA DALTON
> (dabbing sweat from her face)
> Good morning, John! Beautiful day,
> isn't it? What are you making for
> us this morning?

JOHN wipes his hands on his apron.

> JOHN
> Ah, yeah, so what I've decided to
> go with is a classic chocolate
> eclair, very much what you'd see
> in a French patisserie --

> EDDIE TART
> Why a French patisserie?

> JOHN
> Pardon?

> EDDIE TART
> (with a stiff smile)
> Why not an English patisserie?

JOHN glances at the camera and gives an
uncertain laugh. His fingers fiddle with his
apron tie.

                    JOHN
I mean, it could certainly be
found in an English patisserie,
as well. I don't know why I -- why
I specified *French*. I've actually
never visited France, myself.
Never saw any real reason to.

    He clears his throat.

Bit mad, how people used to make
such a fuss about the place.

INT. TENT - DAY

Intensely cheerful music plays as shots
of the CONTESTANTS are interspersed with
shots of the TICKING CLOCK. Faces furrowed
with concentration, dripping with sweat.
Countertops littered with implements.
Hands splattered with chocolate.

                EDDIE TART (V.O.)
    With only half an hour remaining
    in this signature challenge, the
    heat is on! But whose work will
    stand up to scrutiny, and whose
    will topple? Who will emerge the
    champion of chocolate?

EXT. LAWN - DAY

The walls of the TENT sag and ripple. Above it, the sun is a hot white orb in a sandblasted sky. No trace of cloud. The GARDENING BOTS have stopped in place; their metal shells are bright mirrors dotting the green grass.

INT. TENT

SANDRA slides her tray into a freezer, relishing the gush of cold air for a moment before she closes the door. EDDIE TART bounces up to her.

          EDDIE TART
Well, well, look who's the first one done! How are you feeling about it, Sandra?

          SANDRA
     (with a tired smile)
Fingers crossed.

          EDDIE TART
Now, I understand you're from Guildford. But originally...?

PARTIAL TRANSCRIPT FROM THE GREAT BREXIT BAKING SHOW

                SANDRA
         (losing her smile)
I was born in Brighton.

              EDDIE TART
Of course. But your family, originally...?

              SANDRA
My family's from Pakistan, originally. But they've been in England for generations.

              EDDIE TART
Incredible. Incredible. How many generations?

SANDRA stares.

              EDDIE TART
How do you feel about the recent threat of nuclear aggression from the Chinese? I imagine you're worried sick for your many relatives.

              SANDRA
I have to do some more piping, Eddie. On my cake. Sorry.

INT. TENT - DAY

DIANA DALTON and the spheroid are off to one side, watching sweat-soaked CONTESTANTS place their creations in the freezers.

> DIANA DALTON
> Any predictions for the result of this signature challenge, then?

The spheroid deploys its projector, and PAUL HOLOGRAM pops into view.

> PAUL HOLOGRAM
> Handling chocolate is really all about the timing, Diana, and knowing your setting points. I saw a lot of rushing today, and that doesn't bode well.

> DIANA DALTON
> (staring off-screen, eyes wide)
> Oh! Oh, my God.

> PAUL HOLOGRAM
> Feel free to call me Paul, Diana.

The camera pans; we see that one of the CONTESTANTS has collapsed beside their

PARTIAL TRANSCRIPT FROM THE GREAT BREXIT BAKING SHOW

oven. One of their neighbors is splashing water over their face. A PARAMEDIC rushes over, kit in hand.

INT. TENT - DAY

Pale-faced CONTESTANTS remove their baking from the freezers while their fallen fellow baker is stretchered past them. The more delicate creations begin wilting and melting almost immediately. We zoom in on the looks of dismay.

One cake stands out, topped with an ELEGANT CHOCOLATE LATTICE that is somehow withstanding the superheated air.

Tense string music as the CONTESTANTS present their offerings to the JUDGES, one by one. DIANA DALTON takes small, thoughtful bites, and feeds the tiny whirring food processor in the top of the spheroid.

> PAUL HOLOGRAM
> It's got no structure, I'm afraid.
> Just a poor bake.

                    DIANA DALTON
          (faintly, eyes straying to the empty
          counter where the HEAT STROKE occurred)
          The taste is excellent, though.

The next CONTESTANT is SANDRA, who
presents a ganache with a puddle seeping
out from beneath it. She watches in
anguish as the spheroid gnashes down its
sample.

                    PAUL HOLOGRAM
          Bit claggy.

                    DIANA DALTON
          I'm afraid the mirror glaze let
          you down here, Sandra.

SANDRA takes her ruined cake and troops
away, shoulders slumped. The last
CONTESTANT is JANE, a freckly young woman
with blonde hair and a confident air. Her
elaborate chocolate lattice is fully
intact, and EDDIE TART, who has been
watching from the sidelines, beams.

                    DIANA DALTON
          So beautiful I can hardly bear to
          cut it! How did you manage?

PARTIAL TRANSCRIPT FROM THE GREAT BREXIT BAKING SHOW

                    JANE
          Well, I knew it would be tricky
          with the heat -- so instead of
          the cocoa, I used Brit Bars, just
          how my mum always did when I was
          growing up...

Her eyes flick away.

In a rough-and-tumble working class neighborhood.

The other CONTESTANTS murmur in the background shot; some look at the discarded Brit Bar wrappers and shudder.

                    EDDIE TART
          Ingenious! Inspirational! And so
          quintessentially *English*. Judges,
          you'd better have a taste before I
          steal the whole thing for myself.

DIANA DALTON hesitates, then slices off a piece of the cake, which she drops into PAUL HOLOGRAM's food processor. His projected face contorts with disgust, but as he opens his mouth, his pixels jump and rearrange.

> PAUL HOLOGRAM
> (toneless)
> This is fantastic. Great design, great taste, you've really pulled out all the stops, here. If I had a corporeal hand, I'd shake yours.

JANE gives an awkward squeal of delight. The other CONTESTANTS shift nervously. One of them gives a loud sniff. DIANA DALTON, looking faintly ill, lifts her fork and takes a bite.

> DIANA DALTON
> (choking)
> Oh, my. Lovely. Just lovely.

EDDIE TART takes a massive slice and eats with a manic glint in his eye. His smacking lips are the only sound in the tent. Then a CONTESTANT sniffs again, more loudly. Heads begin to turn toward the back of the tent. The camera tracks over to an abandoned oven just as thick dark SMOKE begins billowing out.

An ALARM blares. PAUL HOLOGRAM is panic-stricken.

> PAUL HOLOGRAM
> Not again. Not again! No!

He vanishes, and the clicking spheroid speeds toward the exit. SMOKE is now filling the air. Jagged tongues of FLAME leap from the oven. The countertop catches and is set ablaze as the terrified CONTESTANTS rush for safety. EDDIE TART chews furiously, face pale, determined to swallow his bite of cake. Crumbs spray from his open mouth.

> EDDIE TART
> (howling)
> Delicious! It's delicious, and I have no doubt that you'll be going very far in this competition, Jane, because you've truly captured the *spirit* of what --

EXT. LAWN - DAY, DARKENED BY SMOKE

Aerial view of the rectangular white TENT, which is now a BONFIRE. The show's CONTESTANTS and CREW stagger across the grass. EMERGENCY DRONES converge on the blaze, throwing jets of water into the raging flames. Cheerful music plays.

■

Rich Larson was born in Galmi, Niger, has lived in Spain and Czech Republic, and currently writes from Montreal, Canada. He is the author of the novels Ymir *and* Annex, *as well as the collection* Tomorrow Factory. *His fiction has been translated into over a dozen languages, including Polish, Italian, Romanian, and Japanese, and adapted into an Emmy-winning episode of* LOVE DEATH + ROBOTS. *Find him at patreon.com/richlarson.*

IT TASTES OF ROT

Margaret Roach

Day 40

It has been precisely forty days since I have left my small accommodations due to the declining state of the outside world. Much like the Lord in the desert, I refuse to give in to the temptations of the world around me. I had never thought of my humble, little self as brave, but facing every day is an act of bravery in these wicked times. How good I am for not going outside and staying in my small box of the world! The window tempts me, but I have covered it with a dark black cloth. How smart and resourceful I am! All I know of the outside world is the clanging of pots at 7 p.m. I am content with this fact.

Day 44

I have started to make bread out of decay. It contains flour and yeast. They eat each other to produce bacteria that forces it to rise. It will not be ready to eat for days or maybe even months, but I have no reason to eat it yet. Love is patient and so am I. My Husband (Oh, the honorable Mr. Wright) will be so proud of me! I have placed Bart on our kitchen counter to remind me that something is still living.

Day 48

The bread's name is Bartholomew. When I pour flour into him, he bubbles. I think that it means that he loves me. I love him so much. Before this all began, we had planned on trying for a child, but now the world is too much for that. I have agreed to these terms. I was sad before, but now I am happy. I have Bart and he is all that I need. I hope that he will need me, too. I like to stand in the kitchen and watch him like a mother watching her child in a cradle. I cannot take my eyes off him. I barely breathe at all. I breathe like a bird. I think that it is important for a woman to be as dainty as she could be. If I take in only the smallest amount of air, then I am the essence of loveliness. I breathe in and breathe out.

Day 54

My husband (Oh, the Beautiful Mr. Wright!) returned home today, but he refused to let me kiss him chastely on the cheek due to fears I may become infected with the horrors of the world. How sacrificial he is! Instead, he stood in the shower for three hours and refused to get out. When he left the shower, his skin was red like a warring planet. He laid in bed next to me and breathed in and out. I watched. I love him so much. I think I have always loved him this much. The pacing of my breathing matches his. He was gone when I woke up in the morning; his side of the bed was unmade. I cannot bring myself to make it. I must tell myself: This is how life is meant to be lived.

Day 66

Today, I got a new job. Within hours of sending in my application, I received an answer that I must begin working immediately. My employer's names are the Society Assisting Terrorized Albanian Newts, but they simply call themselves the Society. I have always been a charitable person. They will pay me a wage of eleven dollars and fifty cents. Me and my husband (Oh, the forsaken Mr. Wright!) will be able to worry so much less. He works so hard in the sick wards all night and day. My wage will allow us to buy petty things, like new entertainment and food delivered at night by an unseen figure in a hood. What luck! How wonderful this world is despite the horrors that live in it! My job is so simple. People who complain about jobs are weak-minded.

Day 68

I excel at this job! All I do is write words. I do not know what these words mean because they disappear the moment that I write them down. The words that I catch before they go away are odd. Today, I believe I wrote the word "esophagus" four times. Each time had an extra p. I'm sure it's necessary – we all need to do our part.

Day 70

I think Bart is hungry. All he does is moan. I had to put him into a large bowl because he broke through his glass jar. Flour just isn't enough for him to grow tall. Today, I had a brilliant idea. I took the flies from the sticky trap and slipped them into his supple skin. He's been purring all afternoon! I take care of my son. He is made of flour and yeast. And yet, I feel that he is more than that.

Day 76

I am not lonely, because I have made a dear new friend. He is the man who lives next door. Before this began, I never really considered my neighbors. We lived separate lives in our little bubbles. Maybe we would nod to each other, but they were not complete people. They didn't have interests or lives but were only meant to be faces in the crowd. There are no crowds anymore. The Man Who Lives Next Door is now my dearest friend. Funny how life works that way. I suppose that I have always heard him muttering to himself, but today, I pressed my ear to the side of the bedroom wall. He was speaking to me! What silly things does the Man Who Lives Next Door tell me! He wants me to break all the mirrors, slice through the soft part of my husband's stomach (Oh, the Worthy Mr. Wright!), and go to the grocer to lick all of the red apples. He is so funny!

Day 77

My old self has died and I have become a new, wondrous person. This new woman no longer wears clothes that are stiff, but ones that are soft and contain images of dogs and yellow birds. Her hair is not the color of golden thread, but it has faded at the roots. Her nails are short, and someone keeps biting them off. I barely look in the mirror anymore, but I am sure that this new person is beautiful. She is named Jezebel because it is the name of a queen. I always thought that I was meant to be a queen. As a child, I wore a crown and walked barefoot everywhere. I do not wear a crown, but my shoes have all disappeared.

Day 78

Today, whispered in his slithering voice, The Man next door said, "Jezebel, you must forsake the conveniences of modern life. They have made you fat and lazy. It is not the plague making people sick, but it is modernity. It suffocates them and covers their lungs with a swift black sludge. You can still escape if you begin to live like we used to. Then, you will be ready to be the vessel of our new lord. You were always meant to be a mother." I laughed and laughed! Imagine me – a mother!

Day 87

Batholomew smells of rot. It is the smell of something that has been left in the sun too long or the animal on the side of the road. He is covered in black specks and as I wait for my husband to come home (Oh, My Lost Mr. Wright!), I swear that I can see the specks slowly moving like stars in space. I fed him extra flour today because I am so proud of him. I am a mother. He is my growing boy. Not only am I a mother, but I am also an entrepreneur! I received a promotion at work and now the society has me writing paragraphs. They fade away almost as quickly as the words, but I am able to understand that what I am writing is not about Newts. My boss told me that I am an exemplary employee and that I should expect more things in the world. My promotion is not paid in finances but in secrets gracefully delivered by my sweet friend, The Man Who Lives Next Door.

Today, he has taught me:

1. The past is mostly made of lies created by world governments. We are told stories. There is no truth, only stories so we can live within the comfort of narratives.
2. I am not a human woman. No further context was offered beyond this.
3. My husband (Oh, the Pure Mr. Wright!) was not born of human parents. He was created deep in an underground lab.

I am unsettled by all these things and wish most for a moment of total silence. I beg. The whispering continues. The black specks move faster. They move faster. I remind myself – this is how life is meant to be lived. I am sure.

Day 93

My husband (Oh, the victorious Mr. Wright!) has not returned since his last visit. I receive no communication from him. I miss him, but love is meant to be kept waiting. I keep myself busy. There is work and there is cleaning. After writing my thousands of words of the day, I dust.

Today, I wrote "sin" 330 times. There is so much dust. I read once that dust is from human skin, but it is only me in my home. Where is it coming from? I worry, but it is not a problem. It gives me something to do!

Day 102

Today, I had a conversation with the Man Who Lives Next Door. I have included the transcript. I have no comments.

J: How are you doing, my dear dear friend!

TMWLND: I am not dead. I have always been blessed by the fact that I have not died. Have you looked outside your window lately?

J: No.

TMWLND: Ah, you should! There is a river in the middle of our street and every once in a while, a figure floats down.

J: Are there boats?

TMWLND: No, but there are rafts. There are no people on these rafts. I do not think the water is a good thing. It contains a thick black sludge that is mixed in with everything else. The river smokes.

J: Is that you all see outside your window?

TMWLND: No. I see many things.

Day 115

Bart is starving. He is crying. I can hear the sound of whimpers and I feel an ache in my stomach – hunger or sympathy? I stand in front of Bart in my nightgown. I have never touched Bart. I should not be afraid to touch him. I stick my finger into the fleshy side of him and relish in its coolness. The coolness fades. My hand is sinking deeper and deeper. Teeth! All I feel are teeth. Molars that do not stab, but press and press! So many teeth! I stand in the kitchen as my son bites down. I think that this is what I must do. Finally, I pull my hand out, but it is missing a finger. It doesn't bleed. I don't think it hurts. It aches. That is normal. I'm glad to keep my son alive. I wish he took another finger. That one had my wedding ring on it. Children take so much from us, don't they?

Day 122

Today, a man from the society stopped by my door. He didn't say much, but he wanted to know how Bart was feeling and if he was growing. I had so much to say about Bart! He is a good boy. He is a smart boy. He is all that a mother needs her son to be. I talked and talked for hours. I felt so lonely when the man I left, I just cried and cried. The Man Who Lives Next Door did his best to keep me company. At night, he no longer whispers, but groans. I cannot tell if it is in pain or if it is something else. I fall asleep to the rhythm of his cries. What a good friend.

Day 142

It tastes of rot and sweetness. The bread. It tastes of a warm breath and a mother who needs something to love that is not a child. The heat did not kill the specks of black. It tastes of women dancing naked in fields and accusations. The specks vibrate on the tongue. It tastes of the cold side of the bed and a husband who will not return. The color is not the color of bread. It tastes of a childhood friend who lives a life without you and the metal feeling in your stomach. The specks move faster. It tastes of the world outside the window that has stopped and the sound of pots clanging at 7 p.m. The bread. It tastes of rot and sweetness.

Day 143

Bart showed me things. He showed me secrets, he is helpful in that way. I know everything now. The Society does not protect newts. They protect the future. The world is covered in a thick black sludge and there is nothing left to do except let it start again. Things grow out of decay. They bubble over. I was always meant to be a queen. This will be my chance. What comes after wife? I do. Jezebel. This is who I am meant to be. I saw a picture of myself, or a woman who I assume is me, sitting on a throne covered in black specks with a swollen belly. It is late. My mouth tastes of rot and sweetness. The Man Next Door mutters his praises. I do not sleep, but stare up at the wall. Something moves. Letters appear. I have received another promotion. How proud I am! This is how life is meant to be lived.

Day 150

Today, Mr. Wright (Oh, my beloved Mr. Wright!) returned home. Or, at least I think that he did. A man appeared at my door wearing a hazmat suit and would not stop knocking on my door. I peered into the small, clouded piece of plastic that covered his face, but it was difficult. Most of it was covered in black sludge, but I could see the green of Mr. Wrights's (Oh, my sweet Mr. Wright!) eyes and his ruddy complexion. I opened the door and let him in! I went to kiss and hug him and do all the things that a wife is supposed to do when a husband returns home, but he pushed me away and went into the bedroom. The door is locked. I sit by the door with my knees pulled close to me. The Man Who Lives Next Door won't stop laughing.

Day 170

Bart is feeling anxious. I always know how Bart feels, because a mother understands her son. He does not like Mr. Wright at all. Mr. Wright has started to leave our bedroom and walked around the apartment saying all the things wrong with it. He does not like the way I redecorated. He should have been here if that was a problem. I ignore most of the criticism, it's hard to hear him with the stupid hazmat suit, but poor Bart is distressed. He won't even eat, and he just sits there and throbs. I drop pieces of my left hand into him and the blood just sits there. He's taking on a pinkish hue. It's not how his complexion is meant to be. Something will have to be done.

Day 187

Today, I had a conversation with The Man Who Lives Next Door. I have included the transcript. I have no comments.

J: How are you today, neighbor?

TMWLND: Better than you!

J: Why do you say that?

TMWLND: I do not have an invader in the house.

J: Oh, silly. That's my husband. I love him very much.

TMWLND: How do you know it's him?

J: He's my husband and I love him. Anyway, his eyes are

green. He has always had green eyes. I love this about him because I thought that he had the prettiest eyes I had ever seen. A wife knows her husband's eyes. I am a good wife.
TMWLND: Lots of people have green eyes. I have green eyes and yet – I am not your husband. He is an invader! All he wants is to harm you and the blessed boy. Take off his mask and reveal him! *Moan*.
J: ...

Day 210

I did not have a good day today. Work went on for hours and hours. I have been so busy lately and Mr. Wright (Oh, Mr. Wright?) doesn't appreciate it. He just walks around complaining even when I ask him to go back to the bedroom. He just won't shut up about the kitchen and how much space Bart takes up on the countertop. Men talk so much. Finally, I stood up, walked over, and stared up at his face – was he always this tall? He froze, but underneath the hazmat suit, something was moving. I put my ear to his chest and listened as something buzzed in the suit. He placed a hand on my back and said, "Don't worry Jessica. It will be over soon." I do not know who Jessica is. It is a dreadful name. He says softly like it means something. I do not know how to describe how he said it except that it was soft. I wrapped my arms around his rubber body. My hand goes up. My hand goes down. Something buzzes.

Day 220

I think I might have killed someone today. I say that I killed someone, but I do not believe that the Man In The Hazmat Suit to be my Mr. Wright (Oh, My Lost Mr. Wright!). Despite their shared green eyes, this man tried to murder me, and Mr. Wright would not try to murder me. I was standing at the counter feeding Bart his daily allotment of flesh. I've taken to using a small knife to cut off pieces from my thigh because Bart is greedy and he'll eat too much if he feeds freely. It was too large anyway. I always had fat thighs. I was sliding the knife into the left one and all of a sudden that man was behind me! His hands were around my delicate neck. They were squeezing and squeezing. He was sobbing. He was apologizing. The knife was in my hand, but I couldn't quite get him. He said he had to stop me. He said Bart was an abomination. He said he didn't even know me anymore. God, what an idiot. He shouldn't have mentioned Bart. I am a mother. A mother protects. Bart must live. He is everything. There is nothing, but Bart. I slipped from his grasp and dug the knife into his vinyl chest. I dug and dug and dug. He doesn't move anymore. He lays in the kitchen. The blood will take so much work to clean up. What a nuisance. Bart will be happy at least to have something else to snack on. We all need to try new things.

Day 230
I received another promotion today. Apparently, that man was a sleeper agent who was supposed to destroy Bart and all of our plans. The Society is so proud of me. I even received an employee of the month certificate. It was under my pillow when I awoke this morning. It smells.

Day 242
It tastes of rot and sweetness. The bread this time. It tastes of a whispered proclamation of love and a long, deep moan. The specks have become a black hole. It tastes of red soil next to a playground and a child who may have been. The specks cover my teeth. It tastes of the light fluttering in from black curtains and a cloud of thick dust that grows. The color is pale like a sickness. It tastes of a punch in the gut and a wish for enough pain to go to the emergency room. The specks move faster. It tastes of the world outside that has been consumed by the flood and

the sound of pots clanging at 7 p.m. The bread. It tastes of rot and sweetness.

Day 243

Today, I had a conversation with the man who lives next door. I have included the transcript. I have no comments.

J: Tell me what you see outside your window this morning.

TMWLND: I see apartments like the ones that we live in and people staring outside the window. They clang kitchen utensils for five minutes every hour and have jars of black specks on the windowsill. Do you think they are like us?

J: No. I think they must be very different. They are happy.

TMWLND: They'll all be dead soon anyway. Like your husband. *Groan.*

J: What do you mean? The Blessed Mr. Wright?

TMWLND: There's no need for him anymore. His purpose was to bring you here. All we need is each other, the jar, and The Society. I'm going to be your Joseph *baby. Long moan.*

J: But, what is my purpose?

TMWLND: *Grunt.*

Day 265

Bart loves to eat that Man. He purrs as he eats, and I think he licks his lips. It's sort of cute how excited he gets about his meals. I never thought that I would have a child like this. I thought that my child would wear sneakers and wear their hair in pigtails. Bart doesn't have any hair. I think he'll have a good life anyway. I hope that he does. I'm doing my best here, but there's so little left.

Day 280

Today, the man who lives next door professed his love for me. He has always loved me. He loves me like a man loves a goddess. I liked the things that he said, so I love him, too. Love makes you complete. I am part of a missing piece. We are not meant to be alone. He will be my piece and will be connected at the shoulder and at the hip. Smells of rot and sweetness drift in from the air vent by my bed. I think it's that bad man in the kitchen. He's almost gone now. All that is left is his foot and head. I can't bring myself to look at his face. I coughed and a slick black sludge slipped out of my mouth. It tasted like licking a metal screw, but I was undisturbed. Courage! I whisper over and over again – this is how life is meant to be lived.

Day 300

Today, I received a caller at my door. This caller was not a stranger, but rather my supervisor. "Hello!" I said, my voice coming out a croak. It's like I have never spoken even though I have had many conversations with The Man Who Lives Next Door. "What can I do for you today?" He shudders at my voice. He is such a hard worker. "I need to tell you a secret." "Another one! I really appreciate all the secret telling, but we really must get a move on the whole end of the world thing. Life cannot be all about planning." He smiles. "You are so smart, Jezebel. You always know what I am going to say." I think he smiles. "We need you for the world to end. You need to take the final steps outside your door and let the decay out. You've been so selfish, containing it all for yourself." There are teeth. "You have a destiny, and we always knew that. You always knew that this would be how it ends." "Do I need to do it right now?" "Of course not, we follow you." I watch him and his endless teeth through the peephole. "You are a queen. You just need to accept that." "But, what about the Newts?" He told me not to be stupid and left. Sometimes jobs can be difficult. Still, this is how life is meant to be lived.

Day 306

Bart has begun to reshape himself. I noticed this morning when I was feeding him. He is no longer a pile of dough, but a doughy child. It is like he is made out of clay. I reached for one of his wet, wet hands and we sat on the floor together. I think that I was weeping. There is something wet on my face. It smells like sulfur and salt and iron. Bart doesn't mind if I do not look perfect. All that I am is for Bart. If I was smart, I would be afraid. I am not a smart woman.

Day 308

This is how life is meant to be lived this is how life is meant to lived this is how life is meant to be lived this is how life is meant to be lived this is how life is meant to be lived this is how life is meant to be lived this is how life is meant to be lived this is how life is is meant to be lived this is how life is meant to lived.

Day 310

Today, I had a conversation with The Man Who Lives Next Door. It is as follows. No comments.

J: When will we be married?

TMWLND: When this is all over. We can't get married when we can't leave our housing. We will have to cohabitate.

J: Will you leave me?

TMWLND: I will never leave, you can't leave when you are attached to another person. I'm not a good man, because there is no such thing, but I will not leave you. *Moan*.

J: What do you do for work? I can't believe I never asked you that. Before this, I worked for an advertising company. I don't know what we advertised, but I think that I was happy.

TMWLND: This is all that I've ever been. I was born in the apartment and I've always been waiting for you.

J: Aw, that's sweet.

TMWLND: *Groaan*.

Day 312

You were happy with the world before. It was not the sort of happiness that made you smile or weep with joy, but I think that you were happy with the world as a whole. You and your husband would go on walks. It was a little life. Some lives are meant to be small and lived softly. You would have tombstones that people would take etchings of because they forgot that we once lived. It would be an honor to be forgotten.

Day 314

The Society comes by my door daily and reminds me that I have a duty to start the great reckoning. I signed a contract. I do not remember signing a contract. I do not remember much of those early days. I could have done anything. I remember the first night of this when it seemed like a vacation. This is not a vacation. Queens are always working. Did they forget to ask me what I wanted?

Day 318

Bart took his first steps today. They were much too fast. Children always grow up faster than we want them to. He is getting so tall. He is almost taller than me. Can a mother be afraid of her son? I know that he is meant for terrible things. The green eyes of the man I hate follow me as I move. Lots of people have green eyes. Lots of people have sons who do bad things. All I see is the head of the man I killed, and my son who grows because of me.

Day 320

Today, I had a conversation with The Man Who Lives Next Door. It is as follows. No comments.
TMWLND: Are you ready? *Groan.*
J: ...

TMWLND: This is all you were ever meant to be. Are you ready?

J: ...

TMWLND: *Groan*. This is all you were ever meant to be. Are you ready?

J: ...

TMWLND: You were born in an apartment; waiting. *Groan*. This is all you were ever meant to be. Are you ready?

J: ...

TMWLND: You are a queen. You were born in an apartment; waiting. *Groan*. This is all you were ever meant to be. Are you ready?

J: ...

TMWLND: *Moans*. You are a queen. You were born in an apartment; waiting. *Groan*. This is all you were ever meant to be. Are you ready?

J: ...

TMWLND: You must be ready by now. *Moans*. You are a queen. You were born in an apartment; waiting. *Groan*. This is all you were ever meant to be. Are you ready?

J: ...

TMWLND: We are waiting for you! You must be ready by now. *Moans*. You are a queen. You were born in an apartment; waiting. *Groan*. This is all you were ever meant to be. Are you ready?

J: ...

TMWLND: Are you ready?

(It repeats until his voice is gone. I do not sleep)

Day 333

Was there a life before this? (You used to work in sales.) Did I go outside and breathe deeply? (You used to get drinks.) Did I stare at the sun until it hurt? (You used to think you were happy.) Was there contentment before this? (You used to be a little bored.) Who was I before this? (You used to dream all the time about this.)

Day 342

It tastes of nothing. This has all been nothing. What a silly little woman I am. My husband leaves and I get hysterical! How long has it even been? A week? It must have been the bread. It can have that effect on women, you know. It makes us all crazy and wild. It just needed to ferment a little while longer. I feel so good. I go into the bathroom. I take off my soft clothes and put on my nicest dress. The blue one with little flowers. It does not zip up. Oh, my belly! Still, I look beautiful. I put on mascara. I take off the dress because a woman should always remove one accessory before leaving the house. I remain beautiful. Oh! I will not leave the house, because we all must do our part. Tomorrow, I will quit my job and start a hobby. I don't really need the money. No one has come to collect my bill in ages. The government must be helping. There was a time that I didn't think they were helpful. What a stupid bitch she was! Always complaining about how the world was. That person was an idiot. I am very smart. Tomorrow, instead of praying to the Society, I think I will thank the government. Tomorrow, I will recreate myself again. I will stay inside the box of my world and wait for my friends to come home. Mr. Wright (Oh, Mr. Wright! Oh, Mr. Wright! Oh, Mr. Wright!) has left me, but love fills in the spaces that we leave unspackled. I wave in the mirror. Goodbye, Jezebel!

Day 342 Cont.

It did not taste of nothing. It tasted of rot and sweetness and everything horrible. It has been living inside me this whole time. I am rotting and sweet. Bart has infected me. I was only practice. Used. It is fine. It is for him. I sit at my dining room table. I used to sit here with my green-eyed husband. There is a puzzle on the dining room table. I have never seen it before, it must be from Mr. Wright. I touch one of the pieces and specks consume it. God, men always leave things lying around. It's so much easier without him here. The knocking grows more. Bart is patiently waiting. He wears shorts. What a good boy! He needs to see the world. The Man Who Lives Next Door has resorted to yelling. Oh, silly me! Keeping everyone waiting. A woman must always have things to do. We get silly and bored. Women are so stupid. I am a queen. A queen is not a woman. I cannot believe that yesterday I was so stupid. Even queens are weak. I will not correspond again. Soon, I will get up from the table.

I will walk to the door.

I will open the door.

I will let the rot out.

I am sick of what the world used to be. I am ready for the next one. Oh, I will be so happy. That was not how life was meant to be lived. I do not know how I am meant to live. I will find it. I just have to open the door, but the doorknob is covered in a thick black sludge.

∎

Margaret Roach is a writer who lives and works in the Hudson Valley, New York. She writes primarily speculative fiction about sad robots and unreliable lady narrators. She is inspired by her Catholic school education, her adolescence wasted as a theater kid, and whatever she finds decently funny. Recently, she graduated with her bachelors in English and is now working on completing her masters in Library and Information Science. She works as an evening library assistant who does her very best to not lock people in the library.

CLOWN'S BALLOONS

———————— ■ ————————

Sam Rebelein

The clown stood on the street by her building. He could see her through the window of her corner office. If she'd been on the second floor, or the third (the building had four of them), it could've been argued that the clown was looking at someone else. But because Selene's office was right there on the *first* floor, there were no ifs, ands, or buts about it. The clown was watching *her*.

When Selene arrived in her office that morning, it took her a frozen scared moment to establish that she was, in fact, the intended target of the clown's gaze. He had a sad, skinny face. Sunken and gray and decorated with a red droop of a mouth. He watched her, holding three primary-color balloons by their long white strings. Red, yellow, blue, floating a foot above his head as he stared at her from across the street and through the window.

The clown appeared on Selene's birthday, so after she settled in, she went around the office and asked who sent him. At first, she was amused and slightly alarmed. The clown was off-putting (he never blinked), but it was probably just a birthday prank. She could get to the bottom of it.

By the time she reached Devin (the third person she'd asked about the clown), Selene's amusement had pretty much gone.

"What clown?" Devin asked.

Selene, standing in the doorway to his office, stuck out her chin. "Oh, come on. Are you *all* in on this? The *clown*."

Devin followed her back to her office. The clown did not move. Did not *seem* to have moved while Selene wasn't in view. But as she re-entered her office, Selene could see—from all the way across the street, through the window, and past the five feet that made up her workspace—she saw the clown's eyes flick to hers. She got the sense he'd just been staring at her chair, waiting for her return. And now his eyes would stick to her, the way eyes in portraits follow you through cobwebbed mansions, abandoned asylums, rusted-over amusement parks.

"Freaky," Devin confirmed.

"Right?" said Selene. "He was just *there* when I got in, *still* there when I got back from the bathroom, *and* when I got back from the coffeemaker. He's just ... *there*."

Devin leaned back out of the doorway, called down the hall. "Hey Sahil! You asshole, did you send this clown?"

Taylor appeared in the hall, blowing steam off the top of her mug of green tea. "He's not in yet. What clown?"

"Oookay," said Selene, really over this gag now. "Ha ha. The *clown*. The fuckin ..."

She pointed at him. He didn't move. The daisy in his lapel remained wilty, its petals about to melt away and drip onto the ground. His purple-and-yellow-striped suit jacket billowed a little in the breeze. It was a cloudy February day, and the clown seemed a part of it. As if he'd emerged from the clouds the way rain will. As if he himself were a winter weather advisory.

"The fuck," said Taylor. "Who is that?"

"Maybe *that's* Sahil," suggested Devin.

"It's clearly some white dude," said Taylor.

Although calling the clown "white" wasn't entirely accurate. The skin around his mouth, the wrinkles round his eyes—gray. A doughy, rainy gray.

"I'd recognize Sahil," said Selene. Her arms were now folded across her chest.

"Hm," said Taylor. "Well. Keep me posted."

"Keep you ...?" Selene was aghast. "Nuh uh. Who *sent* this *guy*?"

"You wanna ask Hailey?" asked Taylor. Hailey was the boss.

"It wouldn't be Hailey," Devin said. He laughed. "She has *zero* sense of humor."

This was true.

"Yeah, it's not Hailey," said Selene. "I can tell."

She and the clown watched each other, as if waiting to see who'd draw first.

"Well, if he moves, call security or something," said Taylor. "I have a call, I gotta ..."

"Yeah," said Devin, also retreating. "Hey, happy birthday."

Taylor gave a sharp laugh. Selene did not. Devin and Taylor exchanged a silent *yikes* behind Selene's back, then drifted away to their separate offices.

Selene stood there. She watched the clown. And the clown watched her.

Half an hour later, Sahil arrived in the office.

"What clown?" he asked.

The clown stood vigil for Selene's entire birthday. She nodded at him when she gathered her coat from the back of her chair and left for the day. He stared at her, the same glum expression on his face. His yellow polka-dot trousers and his floppy red loafers not even twitching in the cold of the setting sun.

Selene had watched him through the day, of course, eyeing him the way a mouse will eye a sleeping cat. He had not budged an inch. He hadn't even blinked.

Because the clown was already watching *her*, she figured he wouldn't mind her sliding her phone up out of her lap and taking a picture of him. He showed up in the picture, which was good; he wasn't a ghoul or anything. She thought he might be a statue, but the few people who passed him throughout the day all picked up their pace as they went by, giving him quick looks over their shoulders, giving him wide berths on the sidewalk. Some smiled awkwardly, like they might suddenly be on TV (like, what stunt was *this*?), but most just looked confused and a little spooked.

That's the way you walk by people who are unwell, not random statues. If the clown *had* been a statue, people might stop and analyze it. Pose for pictures with it. Nobody stops and poses with random people dressed like sad clowns, unless they are also slightly unwell.

Furthermore, Selene could *see* the gentle waves of his shoulders, up and down, as he breathed. She figured that was proof enough that he was alive. And she wasn't gonna march out there to *check*. No fuckin way. She very briefly considered running out there and smacking him, threatening to call the police. But, as a Black woman, Selene figured they'd just show up and shoot her through the window, thank the clown for his service. And the clown wasn't harming anyone. Selene didn't see any evidence (yet) that he was a danger to himself or society. He just stood there and watched.

And watched.

And watched.

Whatever, Selene thought, driving home at the end of the day. She still figured it was some dumb birthday thing, whatever it was. She'd been on the verge of buying an office plant anyway, one that she could hang in the window. If the clown wanted to decorate her window instead, he could be her guest. She'd probably learn who the clown was three *months* from now, when someone at an office party would laugh and confess, "Yeah, we were trying to see how long we could keep it going ..." or something like that. "We never told you? Lol oops."

Selene hated office parties.

But no big deal. She'd be laughing about the clown a year from now. Just you wait.

When Selene came back to her office the next day—the clown was still there.

For that entire next day, the clown stood on the corner by her office, watching her. Those same three balloons, red, yellow, blue, clutched in one white-gloved hand. The other hand hung limp by his side. The same floppy shoes. The same wilting daisy. The same drooping, crimson mouth. The same skin that looked like ash about to crumble.

Selene never saw him blink. Never saw him move a muscle. Not once.

"Your buddy's back," observed Devin, appearing in the doorway on that second afternoon. "Find out who it is?"

"Not even a little," said Selene, typing something on her computer, trying to ignore both Devin and the clown.

"You ask Hailey about it?" asked Devin.

"Yes, I did."

"And?"

"She *told* me birthday celebrations were off-limits ever since the new budget restraints, and I should ask *my* clown to leave."

"Huh." Devin ticked his wedding ring against the side of his coffee mug for a moment. "So did you ask him to leave?"

"Devin." Selene dug her fingers into her eyes, rubbed at a Devin-sized ache in her skull, and continued typing.

Devin stood there. "Do ... you want someone to notify security?"

"I *did*," said Selene, typing angrily, loudly, punctuating each syllable. "A*ppare*ntly he's across the street and therefore *off* company property, meaning their juris*dic*tion," slamming a fingernail against the spacebar, "is pretty much *nada*."

An awkward, silent beat.

"Well, okay then," said Devin. "I'll leave you to it."

The clown, on the other hand, did *not* leave.

He never would.

The clown became sort of a friend. Or at least, he spent more time with Selene than anyone *else* in the office. Selene didn't even really consider Sahil a friend, and Sahil was friends with everyone. Ironically, that's what made Sahil so unlikeable to Selene. The clown, however, was a unique and totally silent companion. Every so often, Selene would suddenly jerk around in her chair, glance out the window—but he hadn't moved. Slowly, she'd turn her back to him again, then glance at him in the glare off her screen.

He never even flinched.

After the first full week, Selene found herself saluting him whenever she left the room, telling him not to go anywhere, "I'll be *right* back!" Sometimes in the afternoons, Selene would hit Send on an email, lean back in her chair and stretch her arms up. She'd lace her fingers behind her head and turn to face the clown.

"Long day," she'd tell him. "These fuckin emails. I mean, *you* get it."

The clown did not respond.

After the second full week, Selene began to wonder about the logistics of the clown. For instance, did he wear the *same* yellow pants and the *same* purple jacket every day? Did he have copies, or did he keep washing them? Or did they smell? And that daisy *must* be fake, right? There was no way a live daisy could look *that* wilted for two straight weeks. It must be plastic, must be *designed* to look sad. And the balloons. Surely, he had to have made new balloons by now. Helium didn't last that long. Did it? If they were the same balloons he'd first appeared with, how did he keep them full of helium? How did they float so perfectly?

The clown itself she could forgive. Selene figured you *could* train yourself to remain standing for nine hours a pop, every single day. Monks and, like, samurai probably did that kind of shit all the time. Spartans!

Ancient Spartans *must* have been strong enough to stand completely still, without wobbling or wavering or blinking or sneezing, for entire days on end. It wasn't *impossible*. People were capable of all kinds of things.

But the balloons. What about the balloons?

So Selene bought a pack of balloons. She hadn't really *planned* to. She'd been begrudgingly searching for a card for Devin's birthday (they were both Pisces, old souls) and the balloons had just happened to be there, on an end-cap by the cards. A dollar a pack.

She squished the pack between her fingers, eyeing the clear plastic, making sure she had all the right colors. Red, yellow, blue. At least one of each in there.

Selene brought the pack to the back of the store, to the flowers and big foil balloons, so they could blow up a few with helium. She filled three balloons, red, yellow, blue.

"How long do these latex ones last before they start to sink?" she asked the guy working the helium tank. He leaned against a wall literally covered in balloons, so he seemed like he would know.

"About a day," he said. "The foil ones last ... maybe a week?"

"But not two weeks."

"God, no."

"And the latex ones wouldn't last two weeks."

"I can't see that happening, no."

"Are you sure?"

"Oh yeah." The guy smirked. "I don't clown around about balloons."

This seemed like an intentionally ominous choice of words. Selene said nothing more.

At home, she weighted the three helium balloons to the floor by the wall of her living room. She got a level and marked the tops of the balloons on the wall. Then she took a chair from her dining room table, scraped it across the floor to the opposite wall. She blew up three more balloons, red, yellow, blue, and taped them to the top of the chair, marked their heights on the wall. Her theory was that the clown's balloons were either filled with helium and floated of their own accord (and she *had* seen them bob a little in the breeze, so this made sense). But that meant the clown would have to be refilling them with helium, like, every night. Because unlike the clown's smile or the daisy—the clown's balloons *never* drooped.

Or the clown had somehow fashioned three slim poles to *look* like strings and had tied three breath-filled balloons up there instead. Maybe the balloons didn't float at all, but were designed to *look* like they were.

Selene was beginning to feel like a word problem. *If Selene fills three balloons with helium and three other balloons with her own stupid breath ...*

She felt silly, too, because maybe *this* was the clown's ultimate design. Not to simply spook her at work, but to follow her home as well. To make her question the hows, the whys, the whats. Maybe by fucking with these balloons on her own time, she was playing into his little game, whatever it might be.

I'm not crazy, she told the Selene in the bathroom mirror as she brushed her teeth that night.

Mirror Selene just shrugged at her. *If you say so.*

She lay in bed and stared at the ceiling for a long time. Who could the clown be? What did he want with her? Why was *she* so special?

Selene had never felt special before. And in spite of herself, she *knew* this was part of the reason she allowed the clown to stay. She knew this was why she needed to figure out what his deal was. Because if she could figure *that* out, Selene could figure out why she was suddenly so interesting. *That* felt like a worthy goal.

Selene dreamt she was at a spelling bee. The words were utter gibberish ("Spell *joauhodufben*") but Selene won first place. People applauded her for something she did not understand. In real life, Selene had never won anything. In the dream, she got three blue ribbons.

She fuckin loved it.

In the morning, the balloons had visibly deflated. Selene stabbed them angrily with a pen and threw the rags into the trash.

So, okay, maybe he was refilling them every night. Or filling new ones. Maybe he had an endless supply of *these* specific balloons and was *specifically* fucking with her this way, for some reason she'd never even guess. It could even be someone she'd pissed off in *middle* school, clawing all the way back out of Ms. Pearson's homeroom class to avenge some stupid bullshit Selene had said when she was *thirteen*.

It could be anybody. For anything.

So fine. Whatever. If he wanted to fuck with her, let him have at it. She wasn't gonna give in to his *stupid* guessing game.

But.

How the *fuck* did he keep himself from fucking blinking? For *nine* hours straight, every weekday, for weeks? What mountain did this guy have to climb, what monk did he have to study with for a winter, what ancient *technique* had he had to learn—to avoid blinking?

How? Selene asked him silently through the window. *How do you do it?*

For the clown's third week in Selene's life, she practiced not blinking. After five full workdays of trying, Selene finally managed to blink only thrice all Friday afternoon, and even then, she wept and had to squeeze her eyes shut, had to drink some water, before she tried again.

The only explanation, she decided, was that the clown wasn't human.

Selene did not accept this.

Which is ironic, because the clown was not, nor had it ever been, a human being ...

When the clown had first arrived on Earth, it had gone a *long* time living lonely in the dark. It lived where it'd landed: in a hollowed-out machine works, a few miles up the river from where Selene now sat, watching the unblinking clown through her window. For a long time, the clown fed on nothing but rusted scrap and frozen brick. These were not satisfying meals.

During the day, the clown watched ice float along the river. It watched the trains go by. It didn't understand that the trains were *not* great slithering, whistle-breathing beasts, but were in fact nonliving things, built for smaller, actually breathing people-things. The clown could see these people-things filling the many eyes along the back of the train as it slithered by. The clown thought people were a parasite that lived inside the train. Perhaps they even hurt. Or itched. It took the clown a long summer of watching to understand that people were actually the parasites in charge. This made the clown sad, because it had lost its homeworld to parasites a long time ago.

For a long autumn, each night when the train rumbled in its station, the clown continued to believe that it was a great dragon-thing, snoring as it slumbered peacefully. The clown would make fires out of river-wood, on the concrete floor of the old factory, and it would listen to the snoring of the train, until it, too, drifted off. It would dream of trains, tangling together in a great plain that they ruled. It would dream, inevitably, of home. Mother Clown and Father Clown. And it would dream, again, of the worm-waves, the absolute unfunniest thing to have ever happened to the clown.

The clown would dream, each night, of death.

In the morning, in the harsh of day, the clown would remember that the trains were not in charge of this world, this strange purgatory of granite and cold steel. The clown would remember this, and the clown's frown would grow deeper.

The clown's first companion happened to be a teenage breathing thing who lived in the house on the other side of the tracks. In the winter afternoons, when its parents were not home, this breathing thing would stand in its backyard and watch the ice crack along the river beyond the machine works. It hid a pack of cigarettes under the gas tank of an old grill in the yard, though, of course, the clown did not know "gas" or "grill" or "cigarettes." Nor did it know "Claire," which was in fact, this breathing thing's name. The clown was fascinated by the smoke this young breathing thing blew into the air. Claire looked so lonely. She reminded the clown of the desolation it had fled, far out in the darkvast of space. The frozen waves of worms that had swallowed the clown's home.

Claire did something to the clown's heart, and the clown wanted to be closer to her.

It edged out from the shadows of the machine works. It stood there clutching the balloons that'd carried it from its homeworld, as an orphan and a refugee. The clown watched Claire with the utmost intensity.

Whether the appearance of this clown in Claire's life was the work of a vast engineer in possession of a witty, ironic sense of humor—or whether this was all an absurd coincidence—isn't really the point here. However it happened, the clown *happened* to appear on Claire's birthday. Which really threw Claire off. If it'd come on *any* other day, Claire would have done something im*med*iately. Walked up to the clown, smacked it, shoved it away, yelled at it. "I've already called the cops, you fuckin perv!"

But as it was, Claire believed, in her darkened and scarred heart, that the world was trying to tell her something. Because *here*, a clown had appeared in the barren waste behind her back yard on her freaking seventeenth *birth*day.

Like, fuckin ... geez.

Very nonchalantly, not wanting to disturb this miracle, Claire took a drag off her cigarette. She French-inhaled, then blew a jet of smoke out the side of her mouth.

The clown watched her.

She watched the clown.

When Claire's mother-thing returned from work, the clown slipped back into the shadows. When Claire returned from school the next day, the clown re-emerged. Claire stood there, enjoyed her cigarette, and watched the clown. And the clown watched her.

The two of them enjoyed the most companionable silence Claire had ever known.

Claire had always wanted an imaginary friend. That impulse doesn't go away when you're seventeen, or twenty-seven, or even thirty-seven. It just gets buried better.

But when Claire went off to college the following fall, the clown despaired. In hindsight, Claire knew she should have communicated somehow that she was leaving. Could she have left the clown a note saying not to worry, she'd be back for winter break? *Dear Clown: College will probably suck worse than high school anyway, so let's run off for the circus together. I'm assuming you know where that is. I'll be outside at midnight at your spot. I really hope to see you there. Yours, Claire.*

But it wouldn't have mattered. The clown, of course, could not speak or read any human language.

The clown was so struck by Claire's sudden absence in its life that it wandered out of the machine works for the first time since its balloons had floated it down to Earth. The clown felt sad and lonely all over again.

The Earth was cold and unfamiliar. The clown did not recognize any food it could eat, except the twisted bents of metal along the train tracks, and the rocks along the riverbank. It feasted one night upon a blackened catfish corpse and was very sick. All night, the clown vomited wet ragged mounds of colorful confetti.

The clown swore it would choose its next companion carefully. Someone who showed up *every* day. Someone who sent *all* their emails on time. Not that it understood what "email" was. But the irony of this is clear: If Selene had been a less reliable employee, the clown would never have been drawn to her in the first place.

The clown began to show up outside hair salons. Outside car washes and elementary schools, frozen yogurt shops and bookstores. It watched potential companions through the windows of their workplaces, holding its sad balloons, all red, yellow, blue. It spent a year watching various people, and all of these people shooed the clown away. They threatened the clown, yelling at it in a language it had no hope of comprehending. People spat on the clown, threw things at the clown ... One woman even maced the clown. The clown had feared for an entire night that it would never be able to see again.

By the time the clown discovered Selene, it had made seventeen different attempts at companionship. It had approached Selene with a heavy heart, without much hope. But after a few days, it had allowed itself to rejoice, because Selene did not attack it. She even watched the clown *back*, which brought the clown immense joy.

The clown had sworn it would never be lonely again.

The clown was a thing of its word.

By the end of the clown's fifth week in Selene's life, she'd trained herself to stand erect, her arm extended, balloon-strings clutched firmly in her hand, for nine hours at a time. She'd found a breathing technique that seemed to calm her muscles, which especially worked if she kept her knees unlocked. She'd found clothes online that seemed to match the clown's. The shoes she'd found on Etsy, the jacket and gloves on Amazon, the pants on eBay ... So the outfit could be explained, as could the clown's physical endurance. The balloons she could not quite account for. He was probably buying new ones. Could be special effects. Could be anything under the sun.

But the *blinking*. The blinking was beyond her.

The blinking bothered her.

She was standing in the office kitchen one day, rummaging through the bullshit drawer of random utensils for a plastic fork, when she found the *thing*. She held it for a moment as she worked up half an idea. She brought it home, worked on it a little, and by 9 p.m., Selene had a fully-*formed* idea. It was also an absurd idea. It would likely kill her. But Selene didn't feel like she had much else going for her, other than the mystery of the clown. She did not have a social life. She had no pets, did not speak to her parents anymore. She didn't even have an office plant.

Selene didn't know who to call with her idea, but she felt she needed to call *some*one.

After some debate, Selene called Devin. "Can you drive me to the hospital? I feel weird calling an ambulance on myself."

"Oh my God. What happened?"

"Well, nothing yet."

Devin paused. "So, what, you're psychic now? What's *about* to happen?"

Selene held the ice-cream scoop at eye level. It was the kind of scoop with a blade in the spoon, and a lever on the side you could press so the blade would *shick* around the interior of the spoon. It was supposed to make scooping ice cream easier. Sahil had bought it for the office a long time ago.

Selene had taken it apart, sharpened the blade, and put it back together.

"I'm about to do something *really* fuckin stupid," Selene said.

Selene had not returned to her office for four days. The clown was in despair.

It sat in its sewer-hole each night, gnawing at a chunk of broken glass, wondering what to do. It had been so *sure* Selene was the one for it. So sure that it'd found the perfect companion at last. The clown could spend even more time staring with Selene than it had with Claire. Claire had stared for maybe two or three hours a day. Before Selene had vanished, she had been going the full day, only sometimes blinking. The clown had been in heaven. It was reminded of the days when it had stood around the home-fire with Mother Clown and Father Clown. They would all clutch their balloons and smile at each other. Standing and staring and smiling, for entire days on end.

That had been before the worm-waves came. The worms devoured everything. Every smile the clown had ever known.

But Selene had given the clown reason to consider smiling again. She'd even somehow found the clown's traditional homeworld garb. When she stood there in those floppy crimson shoes, watching the clown through the window, standing and staring *almost* all day, the clown was very happy.

Then Selene had vanished.

The clown, hoping for one last miracle, decided to give Selene three more days (a full week, all told) before it moved on, further down the river. Some other town, some other window. Maybe even *your* window.

But you're lucky, you see, because on that third day— Selene finally made an appearance.

The clown brightened as she came into the office. But she did not come alone. Two other people-things (Devin and Taylor) were guiding Selene into the room. Something was different about Selene's eyes. The clown could not quite see what it was yet.

It watched.

Devin and Taylor led Selene to the center of her office. Selene kept her eyes straight ahead. They were unfocused and glassy. The skin around the eyes was different, too. A strange, drugged smile seemed to tremble about her lips.

The clown watched.

Devin and Taylor let go of Selene and looked at each other. Devin was saying something now ("Whenever you're ready, Heather in HR wants to talk to you about workplace stress and liability ..."). Taylor said something then ("Hailey wants a word, too, I think ..."), but Selene didn't look at either of them. She was looking out the window at the clown.

"That's fine," she said, her mouth moving slow, in a dream. "I just want to know ... Is he out there?"

Devin and Taylor glanced at the clown.

"Yeah," sighed Taylor. "He is."

"He was still showing up when you were in the hospital," said Devin. "Every day."

"Look, we can *call* security," said Taylor.

"No," Selene snapped. "No, don't call anybody. I'm ... happy he's here. I'm happy to ... be here. With him."

Devin and Taylor didn't know what to say to that one.

So they said a few more simple things ("Just yell down the hall if you need *any*thing"), and then they were gone.

Selene stood there, watching the clown. Her eyes were large and empty, her smile confident but insane.

A minute passed.

Slowly, Selene raised a hand. Gently, she waved it back and forth. She kept waving, and as she did, the clown finally realized what was wrong with her eyes.

They were new. They were made of glass.

They didn't fit quite right. They bulged out of her sockets in weird places, and the left one seemed stuck in her skull at an angle, lodged wrong in the socket and pointed sideways. Around the eyes were wide red rings of hacked-up flesh and muscle and bone.

It'd taken Selene a few attempts to remove both eyes. The ice-cream scoop had not been as sharp as she had hoped.

But she was here now, and better for it.

Because *now* she could stand here without blinking.

So she just stood there, smiling, showing her teeth now. Grinning. Waving.

The clown was in awe.

Then the clown noticed something else. It'd been so fixated on Selene's eyes that it had not looked *down*. It hadn't even noticed, until this very moment, that Selene was wearing her full clown garb. The shoes, the gloves, the bright yellow pants and the striped purple suit jacket. Even better, Selene had spent her time in the hospital fashioning a little wilting daisy out of pipe cleaners, in the old tradition of the clown's homeworld.

The clown was pleased beyond measure.

A moment later, Taylor came back into the office.

"You left these in my car," she said, handing them over as quickly as she possibly could, like they might infect her with some alien madness.

"Ohh," said Selene. "Sorry about that. My mind's not ... all *in* today. Hey, is he still here?"

Taylor glared at the clown. "Yeah. He's there."

Selene's smile grew wider. "Good. Good ..." She continued to wave with her free hand. The other held the thing Taylor had brought in from her car.

Taylor left without another word.

She had handed Selene three big balloons. They bobbed a foot above her head. She held their strings tight between her white-gloved fingers.

The clown could not believe its eyes.

The balloons were Mother Clown's favorite colors. Red, yellow, and blue.

This was the happiest the clown had felt in a long, long time.

When Selene showed up the next day, led into her office by Taylor ("But I can't drive you in *every* fuckin day ..."), the clown was even happier. Because now, not only was Selene in the traditional garb of the clown's homeworld, holding those three balloons—she was wearing the traditional make-up that Father Clown used to wear. The bright red gash of a mouth, the dabs of red on the cheeks ... And she was standing there, unmoving, unblinking. Perfect. Just like the old ways the clown had always yearned for.

The clown's frown writhed and turned and became a smile. A big smile. Selene smiled back. And they stood there like that, standing and staring and smiling, for an entire special day.

Selene felt a strange wriggling contentment at knowing she was seen. That she was, for whatever reason, special at last. Special at least for one stranger, anyway. And the clown felt *so* content being in the company of even just a small spectacle of what was once its home. After three shattered worlds, eight million balloon-years, and eighteen failed attempts at human companionship— Selene had helped the clown feel whole again at last.

This was, in fact, a doubly special day for the clown. Because even though every breathing thing that might ever remember this fact had long since been swept away by the worm-waves of a planet many balloon-years away from Earth—today happened to be the clown's birthday.

■

This is Sam Rebelein's third appearance in Bourbon Penn. *He also has work in a variety of publications, including* The Dread Machine, Coffin Bell Journal, Press Pause Press, *Ellen Datlow's* Best Horror of the Year, *and the Stoker Award-nominated anthology* Human Monsters. *Sam's debut horror novel* Edenville *is coming out in October 2023, and his follow-up collection of stories set in the same universe,* The Poorly Made and Other Things, *is coming in early 2025. Sam currently lives in Poughkeepsie, NY, with two very old dogs. For pictures of their sweet, stinky lil faces (and updates about Sam's work), follow him on Instagram @rebelsam94.*

COVER ART

THE REAL WINNIE

───────── ■ ─────────

Bom.K

Born in 1973 in the southern suburbs of Paris, Bom.k fell into graffiti at the age of 17, via the sacrosanct bibles Spraycan Art *and* Subway Art *by James Prigoff, Henry Chalfant and Martha Cooper. Under the influence of the pioneers at the time, he was introduced to the grammar of movement on the walls, vacant lots and trains in his neighborhood, where he multiplied the tags, flops and lettering/character frescoes with strong New York inspiration.*

In 1999, he founded the collective Da Mental Vaporz with Iso and began to produce more personal and intimate graffiti. Padded isolation rooms, nightmarish concrete bars, emaciated B.boys with a sinister look. The universe he develops on huge frescoes is like his world: raw, dirty, violent, peri-urban.

Since then, Bom.k has expanded its infernal bestiary and multiplied artistic experiences outside industrial wastelands. He held his first exhibitions (Paris, Denmark, Los Angeles, Berlin, etc.), published a noted illustration book, and created statuettes, prints and posters that he scattered all around him.

Today, his work focuses on cinemascope format canvases, on which he spreads his imagination, the themes that are dear to him and to cite only one among many others, the famous insane Aerotics, with naked bodies and hybrid sexual chimeras that seem like escapes from a Francis Bacon, plus Gonzo imagery. If stared at long enough, they seem to breathe, come to life, and crawl towards the viewer.

THANK YOU!

PATREON SUPPORTERS:

Jer Blane

Daniel Gardner, HfB

Todd Gill

Brent Jones

Anthony Notarfrancesco

Damon Savage

Peter T. Secker

Tony

Printed in the USA
CPSIA information can be obtained
at www.ICGtesting.com
LVHW041452080823
754338LV00003B/338